el Bond

Comes
Thursday!

Illustrated by Daphne Rowles

Michael O'Mara Books

This edition published in Great Britain in 1994 by
Michael O'Mara Books Limited
9 Lion Yard
Tremadoc Road
London SW4 7NQ

Copyright © Michael Bond, 1966

First published by George G. Harrap & Co. Ltd 1966

A CIP catalogue record for this book is available from the British
Library

ISBN 1–85479–937–1

Printed and bound by Cox & Wyman, Reading

Contents

1 A Mouse with far to go decides to Stay

Mr Peck leaned out of the window in the organ loft cupboard of St Mary's in the Valley and gazed up at the small round object bobbing to and fro in the sky above his head.

'Can't tell what it is, Ma,' he exclaimed, straining to get a better view. 'Blessed if I can make it out at all. Keeps coming and going like.'

'You'll be going if you lean out of the window any more,' warned his wife sternly. 'And then there'll be nineteen fatherless mice in the parish!'

Mrs Peck looked anxiously towards the nineteen members of her family in question, struggling to catch a glimpse of the strange device as it kept appearing and then disappearing again behind the trees which lined the churchyard far below. 'I wish it would make up its mind one way or the other,' she said. 'There'll be a nasty accident soon.'

Mr Peck chose to ignore the remark. 'What do you reckon, Ponty?' he asked, addressing a portly figure hovering behind the supper table. 'You've got good eyesight.'

Uncle Ponty glanced up guiltily from a plate of cheese. 'It looks red to me,' he said, hastily brushing some loose crumbs from his yellow waistcoat. 'Perhaps something's gone wrong with the sun,' he added hopefully. 'A sort of phenomena.'

'It'd be a phenomena all right if it was!' Uncle Washington's voice broke in scornfully from the front of the crowd. 'It's comin' from the west. Sun rises in the east – sets in the west. You can't change nature. Besides, it isn't bright enough.'

'He's right you know,' said Mr Peck decidedly. 'Anyway, the sun doesn't move about like that thing. Hasn't stayed still a second since we first spotted it.'

'If you ask me,' broke in Mrs Peck, before an argument had time to develop, 'we'd better wake Grandpa. He'll know what it is.'

'Wake Grandpa!' Mr Peck glanced towards a crumpled pile of blankets in a far corner of the room and shook his head doubtfully. 'He won't like it. It's bad for his digestion.'

'That thing out there's bad for mine,' said his wife briskly. 'He'll just have to lump it for once.'

'Well, don't say I didn't warn you,' replied Mr Peck gloomily. 'He's only just this minute nodded off.'

'What's that? What's that? Who's nodded off?' The words were scarcely out of Mr Peck's mouth before the blankets suddenly rose into the air and Grandpa Aristide emerged in his wheel-chair from beneath the folds and glared at the other occupants of the room.

8

'What's going on?' he cried, thumping the floor with his stick. 'Where's me ear trumpet? Nobody ever tells me anything. Nobody cares whether I know what's going on or not. Just because I've got my eyes closed and me head under the blankets, doesn't mean to say I'm asleep.'

'There's a strange red thing in the sky, Grandpa,' shouted Mrs Peck soothingly, when quiet had at last been restored. 'And it's coming this way.'

'What's that? What's that? Speak up!' shouted Grandpa Aristide impatiently.

Uncle Ponty pulled a box over to the business end of the conch-shell on wheels which served as Grandpa Aristide's ear trumpet. 'Are you there?' he called as he clambered up.

'Am I there?' Grandpa Aristide rubbed his ear as he glared up at the speaker. 'Of course I am. There's no need to shout. I'm not deaf.'

'I can't see you from where I am,' said Uncle Ponty testily. 'You might have gone out for all I know.'

'Gone out,' grumbled Grandpa Aristide. 'I never go out. Haven't been out for years.'

Uncle Ponty drew a deep breath. 'There's a rather unusual round thing in the sky, Grandpa,' he called, choosing his words with care. 'We were wondering if you have any ideas –'

'What's that? Something unusual in the sky?' Grandpa Aristide peered up at the window. 'Can't see a thing for that blessed great red balloon in the way,'

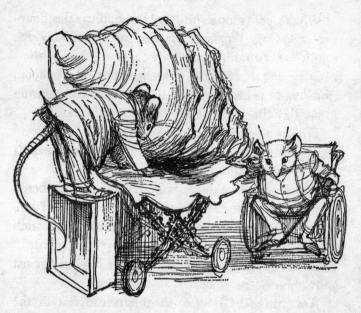

he exclaimed. 'If someone likes to move that I might be able to tell you what it is.'

Grandpa Aristide's words had a far greater effect than even he intended, for as one person his audience turned and gazed open-mouthed at the sight before their eyes.

'A balloon!' whistled Mr Peck. 'See that, Ma? A bloomin' great red balloon!'

'It must have floated nearer while we were talking,' said Mrs Peck, looking impressed in spite of herself.

'Never seen one as big as that before,' exclaimed Mr Peck.

Grandpa Aristide gave a snort as he reached for his

blanket. 'Do you mean to say I've had me post-pran-dials broken into just because of a balloon?' he grumbled.

'If you ask me that's not just any old balloon, Grandpa,' said Mr Peck. 'I reckon it's something special. Look – there's a label tied on the side.'

'And a bag,' added Uncle Washington.

'Looks important to me,' agreed Uncle Ponty. 'I wonder what's in it?'

While the others were talking Mr Peck clambered up on to the window-ledge. 'Chuck us up your um-brella, Washington,' he called. 'I'll see if I can catch it.'

'Careful!' warned Mrs Peck. 'If it hits up against the ivy it might go off.'

Putting their paws to their ears the rest of the family watched in silent awe as Mr Peck tried to nudge the end of the umbrella against the nozzle of the balloon, but a moment later a gasp of disappoint-ment went up as it drifted tantalizingly out of reach again, and then, wafted on a current of air, began to spin in ever-decreasing circles as it slowly gathered speed in a downward direction.

'Pssshaw! That's done it!' snorted Uncle Ponty. 'Your blessed umbrella must have punctured it, Washin'ton.'

'What do you mean, *my* umbrella punctured it?' cried Uncle Washington. '*I* didn't poke the thing.'

'Let's not argue,' said Mrs Peck, pouring oil on troubled waters. 'Let's do something.'

'Quite right, Ma.' Mr Peck jumped down from the window-ledge and licked his paws with relish. 'Let's have some action. Line up everybody. Grandpa – get ready to sound the alarm.'

'I'll read out the code,' said Uncle Washington importantly, as Grandpa Aristide, whose conch-shell also acted as a trumpet in times of emergency, got ready to blow.

'Is all this really necessary?' asked Mrs Peck.

Uncle Washington looked most upset. 'We don't know what's in that bag down there,' he said simply. 'It might be anything. Some of us might not even be comin' back.'

'A Cupboardosity,' he intoned, holding up his paw for silence as a shiver of apprehension ran round the Pecks' living room, 'never flinches in the face of danger.'

'A Cupboardosity,' sang out nineteen shrill voices, 'never flinches in the face of danger.'

'Unless it gets too near,' murmured Uncle Ponty, helping himself to some gorgonzola cheese with the air of one whose every mouthful might well be his last.

'Unless it gets too near,' repeated one or two of the less quick-witted members of the family.

'A Cupboardosity,' continued Uncle Washington, choosing to ignore the unseemly interruption, 'never deserts a fellow Cupboardosity.'

'All for one,' chorused his audience. 'One for all.'

'In sickness,' said Uncle Washington.

'In sickness.'

'And in health.'

'And in health.' The echo of Uncle Washington's words added itself to the mournful sound of Grandpa Aristide's conch-shell and rebounded around the room with such volume and enthusiasm that Mrs Peck reached hastily for the cups and saucers on her dresser in case they should fall and break.

'Wonderful thing edification, Ma,' gasped Mr Peck, rushing to her aid. 'All the same I sometimes wish it wasn't quite so loud.'

'Some of us,' said Uncle Ponty pointedly, 'are playin' for time. What are you, Washin'ton – a mouse or a flea? Why don't you get down below instead of standin' there recitin'?'

Uncle Washington drew himself up to his full height and his face began to go a distinct purple colour as he sought for words with which to express himself.

'For goodness' sake,' exclaimed Mrs Peck. 'If you don't hurry the thing will be blown away and then we shall never know what it was.'

'Either that,' said Mr Peck casually, 'or the Grumblies might get there first.'

Grumblies was the name given by the mice to all humans who hunted them with guns, traps, poisoned bait, and other things too nasty to be mentioned in polite society. The very whisper of the word was enough to strike terror into the heart of even the bravest mouse and as, with a great scampering of feet, the room was suddenly laid bare of its occupants Mrs Peck cast a reproachful look in her husband's direction.

'I didn't say they *would* get there first,' said Mr Peck defensively. 'I only said they might.'

He gave a fruity chuckle. 'You must admit it got 'em moving, Ma. And got 'em back smartish,' he added, as the thunder of many paws grew louder again, only this time with the added sound of something heavy being dragged along behind, bump, bump, bump, on the stairs.

'I should be careful,' warned Mrs Peck, as the leading group of mice staggered into the room and deposited their load on the floor. 'It might be some kind of trap.'

'Perhaps it's food,' said Uncle Ponty hopefully, as Uncle Washington crawled towards the bag and hooked the handle of his umbrella under the string.

'Great steamin' doorknobs!' Uncle Washington suddenly sprang to life almost as if the end of the world was drawing near. 'It's not some*thing* – it's some*one*!'

'Gracious me!' Mrs Peck voiced the thoughts of everyone else in the room as the top of the bag unrolled and revealed another mouse lying there with its eyes closed and its paws across its chest.

15

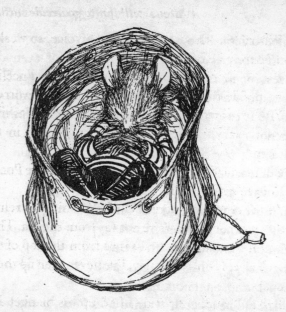

'He's still breathin',' announced Uncle Washington, putting an ear to the recumbent figure.

'We'd better get him on the couch,' said Uncle Ponty. 'Stand back everyone and give him some air.'

'Where on earth can he have come from?' asked Mrs Peck.

'Looks sort of foreign to me,' said Mr Peck, as he helped lift the body. 'Foreign and yet not foreign, if you know what I mean.'

'Ssh!' Mrs Peck silenced her husband with a wave of her paw as a faint stirring came from the figure on the couch. 'I think he's coming round. Perhaps he wants to say something.'

'Where . . . where am I?' asked a voice, so weak it could barely be heard.

'You're among friends,' said Mr Peck, kneeling down beside the couch. 'There's no need to worry.'

'You're in an organ loft,' explained Uncle Washington. 'St Mary's in the Valley. It's a church in the country.'

'But not far from the sea,' interrupted Uncle Ponty, anxious to get a word in.

'As the crow flies,' agreed Uncle Washington reluctantly, 'you could say we're not far from the sea. They do say it's possible to see France from the top of the church steeple on a clear day. I've never been up there, of course.'

'Pah!' Grandpa Aristide lifted up his blanket and gave a loud snort. 'If you all talk at once the lad won't know whether he's on his head or his heels,' he exclaimed.

'Can you tell us your name?' asked Mrs Peck gently, as the mouse sat up and looked around the circle of faces in great surprise.

'1397869,' replied the visitor promptly.

'1397869?' repeated Uncle Washington incredulously. 'That's not a name – that's a number.'

'That's all we had where I come from,' explained the mouse in a stronger voice. 'There were rather a lot of us in the Home so we didn't have any names – only numbers.'

'The Home?' echoed Uncle Ponty.

The Pecks' visitor nodded. 'The Home for Waif-mice and Stray-mice. I didn't like it there very much so I escaped.'

The Cupboardosities looked at him with renewed respect. 'I've heard of that place,' said Mr Peck. 'Miles from anywhere. Mean to say you came all that way by yourself on a balloon?'

'Not *all* the way,' said the mouse. 'I had to dig a hole under the wall first, and then I got inside a Grumbly's lorry, and that took me to a Fair. After I'd had a ride on the roundabout and things, I found the balloon. I think there was a sort of race on . . .'

'He's right you know,' said Uncle Washington excitedly. He held up the label which had been tied to the side of the balloon. 'It says here *"Please fill in your name and address and return immediately saying where found. A prize will be awarded to the finder of the balloon which travels the greatest distance"*!'

'A balloon race!' Mr Peck gave a long low whistle as a buzz of excitement went round the room. 'Fancy – and we've found it.'

'It had got stuck in a tree,' explained their visitor, 'so I climbed up and tied my bag on the side and jumped in . . . and . . . and here I am. It wasn't very difficult.'

'It wasn't very easy either by the sound of it,' said Mrs Peck, amid general agreement. 'What about your family? Won't they be worried?'

The mouse looked most surprised at the question.

'I haven't got any family,' he replied simply. 'I was found on a doorstep.'

'No family!' The Cupboardosities looked at each other in consternation.

'We'll soon put an end to this state of affairs,' said Mrs Peck decidedly. 'You can come and live with us. One more mouth to feed won't be a disaster. That is,' she added, 'if you'd like to be a Cupboardosity.'

'A Cupboardosity?' echoed the mouse doubtfully.

'That's a mouse who lives in a cupboard,' explained Uncle Washington.

'An organ loft cupboard,' added Uncle Ponty. 'Don't forget that. Most important.'

'Sometimes you'd help in the shop,' said Mr Peck.

'And sometimes in the house,' added his wife.

'We all take it in turns,' said Uncle Ponty.

'Most of us,' interrupted Uncle Washington meaningly. 'Some of us take more turns than others.'

'In the summer we go fruit-picking,' said Mr Peck hastily. 'Storing up things for the winter.'

'Strawberries,' said Uncle Ponty, drooling at the thought. 'And in the autumn it's nuts and blackberries.'

The mouse thought for a moment, still hardly able to believe the sudden change in his fortunes. 'It sounds very nice –' he began.

'T,' broke in Mrs Peck. 'If he stays he'll have to have a name and it must begin with "T".'

'Ma always likes to have her children named

alphabetically,' explained Mr Peck. 'It's much less trouble in the long run.'

'I'm Aristotle,' said the tallest of the Pecks' offspring, holding out his paw. 'I helped carry you up the stairs.' He pointed to the row of eager faces behind him. 'This is Blaze and this is Cadwallader. Behind him there's Desdemona, Ethel, Francesca, Gaston, Hildegard, Iolanthe, Justin and Kean.'

'And I'm Ludowick,' the next mouse in the line stepped forward as Aristotle paused for breath. 'And this is Mordecat, Napoleon, Osborn, Peregrine, Quentin, Rowena and Sylvester.'

'We can't stop being alphabetical now,' began Mrs Peck. As she spoke she glanced up at the window and then raised her paws in horror.

'Mercy me!' she cried. 'Just look at the sun. It's right overhead. It must be long past our bedtime. If we don't get some sleep we shall never be able to work tonight.'

'You're right, Ma.' Mr Peck stood up and gave his braces a loud thwack. 'It's all this talking lark,' he said, stifling a yawn as he turned to their visitor. 'I'm afraid you'll have to go without a name for the time being. Never mind, we'll think of something.'

'Some people grow to look like their names,' said Uncle Ponty darkly, getting ready to leave as the rest of the family scattered and began pulling out bunks and unloading blankets in preparation for bed. 'Can't be too careful.'

'Look at Aunt Lettuce,' agreed Uncle Washington, helping the other on with his coat. 'Got to the stage lately where the old girl never goes out. Just sits there, moping, in that salad bowl of hers.'

Mr Peck gave another loud yawn and stretched himself as he led the visitor to a vacant bunk. 'Park yourself down here,' he said. 'Ma'll get you something to eat before you go to sleep. We'll give it another think later on.'

'How nice to have someone young about the house again,' said Mrs Peck, as her husband rejoined the others. 'With all the children growing up so fast I do believe we were beginning to get a bit stodgy. It feels different already. I do hope he stays.'

Mr Peck nodded. 'We shan't forget this Thursday in a hurry,' he said, surveying the happy group on the other side of the room. 'It's been a Thursday to remember all right!'

'Thursday!'

To everyone's surprise, Grandpa Aristide, who had been sitting under his blanket recovering from his exertions with the conch-shell, suddenly came to life. 'Thursday,' he boomed. 'That's it. Very good name. Don't know why no one thought of it before.'

'*Thursday!*' exclaimed Mrs Peck in surprise.

'Thursday.' Mr Peck repeated the word several times and then sat down savouring the result as he might have savoured a sample of cheese from his shop. 'Do you know, I believe Grandpa's right, Ma.'

'Right? Of course I'm right!' Grandpa Aristide, who wasn't always quite so hard of hearing as he liked to make out, glared at the assembly. 'Suits him. He looks like a Thursday. Begins with a "T" as well. What more do you want?'

'Thursday's child has far to go,' said Uncle Washington knowledgeably. 'Sounds very suitable to me.'

'You can put HON. CUB. (TEMP.) after your name if you do decide to stay,' put in Uncle Ponty. 'That means you'd be an Honorary Cupboardosity.'

'Only temporary of course,' warned Mr Peck. 'Until everything's decided properly like.'

'But entitled to all the benefits,' added Uncle Washington. 'Just like one of the family, am I right?'

Mr Peck nodded.

'If you stay for good,' said Mrs Peck, 'you might even become a full Cupboardosity one day. There's no reason why not.'

'You'd have lots of adventures,' said Aristotle, speaking up for the others. 'We're always having adventures.'

'*Please* stay,' chorused the rest of the family.

Their visitor thought for a moment. The combination of the long journey, the warmth and chatter in the organ loft cupboard, and the sight of all the friendly faces around him, were beginning to have their effect.

'I think,' he announced at last, amid a burst of cheering from the younger members of the family, 'I would like to be a Cupboardosity called Thursday very much indeed. Especially,' he added as an afterthought, 'if I have lots of adventures. I like adventures.'

2

Thursday makes a Friend and a Hunting they do go

'The world,' said Uncle Washington at dinner several nights later, 'the world is like an oyster-shell. Open it and what do you find?'

'An oyster,' said Uncle Ponty, licking his lips.

Uncle Washington clucked impatiently. 'Sometimes,' he said with dignity, 'you find a pearl.'

'A *pearl*!' echoed Thursday, looking most impressed.

In the short time that had passed since his flight from the Home for Waif-mice and Stray-mice and his initiation as an honorary member of the Cupboard-osities, a great change had come over Thursday. His fur had lost its bedraggled look, his whiskers had taken on a new gloss and springiness, and he was also looking decidedly fatter; a fact which met with Uncle Ponty's whole-hearted approval.

'Have another biscuit,' he said, pushing a plate across the table. 'Much more interestin' than pearls. Can't eat pearls. Nasty things. Get stuck in your throat and give you indigestion.'

Uncle Washington frowned. 'All I'm trying to say,' he continued, 'is that things aren't always what they

seem. Life is what you make it. Let things get the better of you and the skies will come tumbling down about your ears. Go out and meet it half-way and there's no knowing what may happen. Thursday asked what the world is like and I'm trying to tell him.'

'It's not a simple question,' agreed Uncle Ponty.

'There are as many answers to a question like that,' said Uncle Washington, looking mollified, 'as there are stars in the sky.'

'Or pips in a barrel of strawberry jam,' added Uncle Ponty. 'The world is made up of earth, of rocks and stones, trees and bushes, rivers and lakes, ups and downs, ins and outs. It's flat and yet it's not flat . . .'

'It's round,' interrupted Uncle Washington. 'Like a ball.'

Uncle Ponty looked pityingly across the table. 'Anyone who believes the world is round,' he said, 'will believe anything and deserves to fall off it the very next time he takes a wrong turning.'

Uncle Washington took a deep breath. 'Down at the library where I live,' he said ponderously, 'there is a thing called a globe and it's round.'

'And what happens to the things on the bottom?' asked Uncle Ponty. 'Why don't they fall off? What about all the water in the sea? It must be flat. Stands to reason. Anyone who thinks otherwise is a fool.'

'If you really want to know what the world is like,'

Thursday,' said Mrs Peck hastily, 'I should ask Harris.'

'Good idea, Ma,' agreed Mr Peck, butting in to the conversation. Arguments between Uncle Washington and Uncle Ponty were inclined to go on and on and in the past had sometimes been known to continue for days. 'You can take him his groceries if you like. He's due for a delivery tonight.'

Mr Peck kept an Exchange and Mart Food Store in the nearby village which was patronized by most of the mice in the district and it had been decided that Thursday, like the rest of the family, should serve his apprenticeship in the trade for the time being.

'Harris lives by the river,' explained Mrs Peck, 'so he sees a lot of the world.'

'Inquisitive things, them voles,' said Mr Peck. 'Still, he's a good customer, I'll say that for him. Always pays his bills promptly, that's what I like.'

'Bits of information keep floating past,' said Mrs Peck, 'and Harris collects them.'

Uncle Ponty gave a shudder. 'Have you seen some of them?' he asked. 'Don't know as I'd like to have 'em within fifty miles let alone give them house room.'

'Waste not – want not, that's Harris's motto,' said Mr Peck, bringing the conversation to an end as he wiped his plate clean with a morsel of bread. 'Anyway, he can't help being short-sighted.'

With that Thursday had to be content, but shortly

afterwards, feeling very important, he mounted his delivery cycle and pedalled off in the direction of Harris's hut by the river-bank.

After a day of sunshine it was a cold, crisp night with just a hint of mist in the hollows of the ground and he was glad when at long last his eyes made out the dim shape of a tin hut standing to one side of the road behind a clump of bushes.

A small but reassuring chink of light came from a crack in the wall on the side nearest the stream, but when he knocked it went out. Then for several moments there was silence until he suddenly became aware of some heavy breathing nearby and an eye staring at him through a hole in the door.

'Groceries,' said Thursday promptly.

'You're new aren't you?' asked a voice suspiciously.

'Fairly new,' said Thursday. 'I only started this week.'

There was another short pause followed by a rattle of chains and the sound of a bolt being withdrawn and then the door slowly opened.

'You must be Thursday,' said the owner of the voice from the darkness beyond. 'I've heard about you. I'm Harris. "H" for Harris. "A" for Arris. "R" for Ris. "R" for Ris. "I" for Is –' The voice broke off suddenly and there were several bumping noises followed by some muffled exclamations and a loud scratching sound.

'Sorry about that,' said Harris apologetically, as a match spluttered alight. 'I'm afraid I haven't got many mod. cons. here.'

Harris applied the match to a nightlight which stood in a saucer in the middle of the floor and by its glow Thursday made out a small room which seemed to be filled from floor to ceiling with an almost indescribable amount of junk. Pieces of wood, bundles of paper, tin cans, string, wire, old paint brushes long past their best, clothes, were all piled higgledy-piggledy on top of one another in a most precarious fashion.

Pushing his way through the mounds of rubbish Harris led Thursday towards a relatively clear corner of the room where there was a bed which seemed to be made up almost entirely of old newspapers, several boxes of various shapes and sizes which served as cupboards, and a long table made out of a piece of carved driftwood to which some legs had been added.

Harris held out his paw. 'Pleased to meet you,' he said warmly. 'Sorry about the business with the door just now. Can't be too careful though – especially at night – what with the rats and the foxes . . .' While he sorted out a spare box for Thursday to sit on, Harris went into a graphic description of the awful things that could happen to anyone foolish enough to open their front door without first making sure that all was well.

'A couple of shakes of a fox's tail and you're a goner,' said Harris, giving a shiver. 'And if it's an owl . . .'

'Why do you live here?' asked Thursday with interest.

'It's so nice and peaceful,' replied Harris vaguely. 'Especially in the summer. Good,' he exclaimed, as he began unloading his groceries, 'you've got some bread. I need that for my bait.'

Harris turned and eyed Thursday with interest. 'I say, do you like fishing?'

'I don't know,' said Thursday. 'I don't think I've ever tried. I've never really been out in the world before.'

'You must come over and have a go some time,' said Harris carelessly. 'It's great fun. I've got plenty of spare rods. Tell you what, bring some sandwiches and lemonade and we'll make a day of it.'

'What do you catch?' asked Thursday innocently.

'Catch?' For some reason Harris seemed to find the question annoying and for a moment he looked almost cross. 'You don't have to *catch* things to enjoy fishing.'

'I only wondered if you ever caught any oysters,' said Thursday hastily, and he went on to explain about the conversation he'd had with the uncles earlier that evening.

'I don't think you'll find any round here,' said Harris slowly. 'Old boots, a minnow or two, bits of weed, but I've never seen an oyster. Oysters live in beds, not streams.'

'Beds?' repeated Thursday, looking most surprised.

'That's right,' said Harris. 'Beds. I remember reading an article about it one night before I went to sleep.'

He hurried across the room, removed several fishing-rods from his bed, and began searching through the pile of old newspapers and magazines.

'Now, where was it? I can't remember whether I was lying on my stomach looking down or on my back looking up.

'Ah, here it is!' He reached over the bed and pulled out a large sheet of coloured paper. 'I must have been on my back looking sideways.'

Thursday waited patiently while Harris settled himself near the nightlight and prepared to read.

'Urggh bromskold,' said Harris slowly after a moment or two. 'Cringe yrfdog yackydo. That's funny. I don't remember reading that before.'

'There's a picture on my side,' said Thursday, 'and it's the wrong way up.'

Harris gave a start. 'Fools!' he exclaimed crossly. 'You know what they've done? They've printed everything upside-down! I don't know how they can expect people to read properly if they do things like that.

'Ah, that's better,' he continued, turning the page round. 'There's a picture and everything. Look – it says "a typ-ic-al oy-ster bed".'

'It doesn't look very much like a bed to me,' said Thursday, peering over Harris's shoulder at a picture of what seemed to be a large expanse of water.

'That's because you've never seen one like it before,' replied Harris promptly. 'You can't go by names. Things aren't always what they seem, you know. I know a place where they've got so many different kinds of beds it would make you dizzy trying to count them all.'

'Wouldn't it be nice,' said Thursday dreamily, 'if we really did find a pearl. I wish we could go and look for one.'

Harris looked slightly taken aback. 'Now?' he exclaimed. 'Tonight?'

'Why not?' asked Thursday. 'Uncle Washington says you have got to go out and meet these things half-way otherwise they never happen.'

Harris seemed unimpressed by this piece of information. 'I haven't noticed Uncle Washington going out and meeting things half-way very often,' he said. 'He doesn't have to brave the dangers of the night.' Once again Harris began to wax lyrical on the subject of being out in the dark and then suddenly, for no apparent reason, he changed his mind, blew out the candle, and beckoned.

When his eyes had grown accustomed to the darkness Thursday followed his new friend out of the hut and together they made their way along the road in the direction of the village.

33

Harris strode on ahead leading the way, seemingly in high spirits once again. He was humming a gay tune to himself and Thursday was hard put to it to keep pace.

At long last, however, they stopped by the side of a tall building with very large windows and, after looking round to make sure no one was watching, Harris disappeared through a grating. He led the way along a ledge, through several more holes, and finally came to a halt on the other side of one of the windows.

'There!' he said, as Thursday joined him. 'What do you think of that?'

Thursday's eyes grew larger and larger as they took in the scene before them. There were beds everywhere. Long beds. Tall beds. Short beds. Wide beds. Beds towering up into the darkness like huge mountains. Beds leaning against walls. There were so many he soon gave up trying to count them all and instead he turned to Harris.

'I didn't think there could be so many in the world,' he admitted.

'If we don't find a pearl here we never shall,' said Harris. He pointed towards one row which stretched away into the distance like a line of soldiers on parade. 'Come on – you take that side – I'll take this. See you up the other end . . .'

Harris's voice trailed away as he disappeared into the darkness. 'Hurry up,' he called. 'We haven't got all night.'

But Thursday was hardly listening. Instead, he was staring wide-eyed at a small white object on the floor which lay caught in a shaft of moonlight shining through the shop window.

Harris's voice drew near again. 'Come on,' he said, impatiently. 'Don't just stand there. This shop belongs to some Grumblies. We don't want to be here in the morning when they open up.'

'Look,' whispered Thursday. 'You don't think . . . it couldn't be . . .'

Harris caught his breath. 'Some people,' he said, 'are born under a lucky star.

'Some people,' he said, 'could fall off a two-hundred-foot cliff and land on a pile of feathers.

'Some people . . .'

'You think it really is a pearl?' asked Thursday, still hardly able to believe his eyes or his good fortune.

Harris picked up the object and held it up to the end of his nose as he examined it carefully under the light. 'One of the largest I've ever seen,' he announced confidently. 'Perfectly shaped.'

'I've only seen pictures, mind you,' he added hastily. 'But if you want my opinion . . .'

'Let's go shares,' said Thursday generously. 'I'd like to, really I would.'

Harris shook his head. 'Findings keepings,' he said. 'You have it. It was your idea in the first place. Besides, it's a bit grand for me and you may be glad of it one day.

'I tell you what,' he added, as he saw the look of disappointment on Thursday's face. 'If you really want to do something to please me, how about coming fishing one afternoon? There's a new sort of bait I want to try. Bread pellets mixed with treacle. It'll be great fun.'

Harris led the way back out of the shop and then they both stood for a moment on the pavement looking up at the sky.

'I see what Uncle Washington meant about the stars,' said Thursday. 'There are a lot.'

Harris nodded his agreement and then gave a shiver as he pulled his blazer up round his neck. 'I don't know about you,' he said, 'but I'm for bed.'

Thursday paused for a moment in order to take one last look at the Heavens and then followed his friend.

'You know,' he said thoughtfully when they were together again, 'this must be my lucky week.'

Harris waved one paw vaguely at the sky as he led the way back up the street. 'It's as I was saying,' he remarked. 'Some people are born that way. Some people are born under a lucky star. I expect if you look hard enough you'll see yours somewhere up there.'

*

Later that night, towards morning, when the first rays of the sun filtered through the trees on the hill in front of St Mary's, Thursday lay safely tucked up in bed, a contented smile on his face. By his side, in a place of honour, stood the small round object he'd brought home in great excitement just an hour before.

'Think we ought to tell him, Ma?' asked Mr Peck.

'Certainly not,' said Mrs Peck. 'Not on his first night out. It would be a shame to disappoint him.'

'After all,' said Uncle Washington, 'what *is* a pearl?'

'Something round and white,' replied Uncle Ponty. 'Something precious.'

'And what is a collar-stud?' asked Uncle Washington, looking at the object beside Thursday's bed.

'Something round and white,' repeated Uncle Ponty.

Uncle Washington nodded. 'Exactly. And to someone who has very little a collar-stud, even a broken one, can be the most precious thing in the world. Things are as valuable as you like to make them and beauty is in the eye of the beholder. All those in favour of keeping it a secret say "aye".'

A chorus of 'ayes' greeted Uncle Washington's speech and for once the loudest 'aye' of all came from the lips of Uncle Ponty.

'I don't often agree with you, Washin'ton,' he whispered, tip-toeing away from the bed as the noise caused Thursday to stir in his sleep, 'but, by Jove, I do tonight.'

3   Harris
spins a Yarn . . .

Now that he'd started work in earnest, Thursday's life suddenly became very full.

Mr Peck's Exchange and Mart Food Store in the near-by village was an old-established business which had been in the family for many years and had been presided over, on and off, by countless generations of Pecks.

Mr Peck himself had been born and brought up in London, serving his apprenticeship to the trade with a large firm of cheese importers. It was there that he'd first met Mrs Peck and when, shortly after their marriage, he'd suddenly inherited the family business, they'd both come to the village to live.

Under Mr Peck's guidance, and with his expert knowledge of cheese, the business flourished as never before, and its fame spread far and wide, until it became the mecca of bargain-hunting mice for many miles around.

But fame brought its worries. Even with nineteen children helping in the shop Mr Peck was often hard put to it to satisfy his many customers and provide the service to which they had grown accustomed. So Thursday soon found himself plunged into the thick of things.

If he wasn't on his cycle carrying out errands or

delivering groceries he was busy polishing counters, sharpening knives, or sprinkling sawdust on the floor of the shop before the first customers arrived.

It was enjoyable work and he wouldn't have missed a minute of it, but all the same, whenever he had a spare moment he hurried down to the small tin hut by the stream in order to visit his friend Harris.

Together they spent many happy hours fishing, talking, or simply lying in the long grass watching the world go by.

Harris was a great talker when he was in the right mood and his conversation, although it occasionally took Thursday by surprise as it darted off at a tangent, ranged over many subjects.

He dropped one such remark quite casually, one evening some weeks later, as they sat by the stream before Thursday set out for work.

Harris, dressed as if for an outing, in a straw hat and blazer, was fiddling with a tin of bait on the bank when he suddenly looked up and asked Thursday if he liked birds.

Thursday stared at the gently flowing water for a while before he replied.

'I like some birds,' he said cautiously, 'and I don't like others. The ones that don't peck are all right, I suppose.'

In his heart of hearts Thursday didn't like birds at all, particularly when they flapped their wings and fluffed up their feathers so that they grew large and fearsome.

Harris greeted his reply in silence and for a moment or two busied himself with a piece of cotton which he was tying to the end of a long stick. After a while he appeared satisfied and with a whirl of the stick above his head cast a small white pellet, which he'd attached to the other end of the cotton, fairly and squarely into the middle of the stream.

While all this was going on Thursday put his paws behind his head and stared up at the sky. All around him the countryside throbbed and hummed as millions of creatures went about their daily work.

'What a lot of things there are going on in the world,' he said.

Harris nodded. 'The quieter you are the more you hear. Especially in the summer. I often lie on the bank and count the sounds. When you're like me and you can't see very well you get to know them. I counted one hundred and fifty-six one day.'

'One hundred and fifty-six?' echoed Thursday, looking most impressed.

'All different,' said Harris. 'Mayflies, butterflies, gadflies, horseflies . . .'

'Bees,' interrupted Thursday. 'I can hear a bee . . .'

'That's a bumble bee,' said Harris knowledgeably. 'Then there are the workers and the drones. Ants, earwigs, mosquitoes, fish biting, aeroplanes, cars, bicycles, dozens of different kinds of beetles, wasps . . .'

'Birds,' said Thursday. 'There are lots of birds.'

Harris fell silent for a moment. 'I know a bird that's being kept prisoner in a wooden box,' he said suddenly.

Thursday rather wished he'd thought of some other creature to add to the list. 'Perhaps it likes it in there,' he said.

'I don't think so, judging by the noise it makes,' replied Harris. 'If you ask me it's being tortured.'

'Tortured!' Thursday sat bolt upright and stared at his friend.

'Day and night. Night and day. But it's always worse at night. The screams . . .' Harris gave a slight shudder, leaving the rest to Thursday's imagination, and then dropped his voice to a whisper. 'He's in a Grumbly's house just up the road. I was there one night – just as the church clock was striking twelve. The light was on so I saw it all with my own eyes. He came out of this hole and nearly shrieked the place down. Then a hand pulled him back in. Gave me a fright I don't mind telling you.'

'A hand,' breathed Thursday. 'Was it a big one?'

'Well, I didn't actually see it,' admitted Harris. 'But something pulled him back in. And then there was this noise of machinery and the door slammed shut.'

Thursday gulped. 'Did you . . . did you see him again?'

'No fear,' said Harris. 'I didn't stop for any more. The noise!'

Harris cupped his paws to his mouth and gave vent to an ear-splitting shriek which echoed and re-echoed about the clearing. For a moment it seemed to Thursday as if everything in the world had stopped in sympathy and the only sound to break the silence was the beating of his own heart.

'It was something like that,' said Harris simply, 'only much worse!'

'What are we going to do about it?' asked Thursday in a whisper.

'Do?' Harris looked most surprised at the question. 'Leave him, of course. Probably serves him right. Nasty things, birds.'

'But you can't *leave* him,' exclaimed Thursday.

'I jolly well can,' said Harris. 'I don't suppose you'd get any thanks if you did save him. Probably peck you into the bargain.'

'You don't know that he would,' said Thursday. 'He might be very grateful.'

'Pigs might fly,' said Harris, looking as if he was beginning to wish he'd never brought the subject up.

'You haven't been a prisoner,' said Thursday. 'It's awful when you want to escape from something.'

Harris maintained a stony silence while Thursday sought for some way to express his feelings.

'Supposing ... supposing it was a bird that liked fishing. Supposing it was shut up there for the rest of its life and could never hear the sound of a stream again, or see a fish jumping in the water, or ...'

'It wouldn't be easy,' said Harris thoughtfully. 'The trouble is they've thought of everything.

'First of all, there's the problem of getting into the prison itself. It's very high up on a wall. There's a door underneath. It's only a glass one but it's quite big. As tall as that blackberry bush over there.'

Thursday followed the direction of Harris's paw until his eyes came to rest on a large bush which seemed to tower above all the others in the area.

'Well, perhaps not quite as big,' admitted Harris, 'but we shall need levers to open it with. And then, when we get inside, there are the chains . . . and when we've climbed those there are the cogs . . .'

'Cogs?' repeated Thursday.

'Big shiny wheels with spikes on,' explained Harris with relish. 'Dozens of them. Going round and round all the time. Catch your whiskers in one of those and that'll be the last you'll see of them. They'll be ground up into so many bits you won't be able to count them all – that is if you're lucky and they're pulled out by the roots. If they're not . . .'

Thursday shivered. There was a bloodthirsty side to Harris's nature which didn't always appeal to him. 'If you don't go, I shall go by myself,' he said bravely.

Harris looked at him. 'Who said anything about not going?' he demanded. 'It's when we get past the cogs that the trouble's going to start,' he continued. 'Inside the box itself. We don't even know what we shall find in there.'

'It's early-closing day in the shop today . . .' began Thursday.

'Now's the time, of course,' said Harris, the light of battle shining in his eyes. 'The Grumblies are all away at the moment. Saw them drive off two days ago with their luggage. Gone on holiday I shouldn't wonder.'

Thursday stood up. 'I'd better tell the rest of the family,' he said. 'We may need some help.'

'Tell them to bring plenty of food and drink,' said Harris. 'We may be there some time. I'll bring some bits of wood and some string. And some bandages – just in case . . .'

'I'd better go,' said Thursday, as Harris's list of

their various wants began to grow. 'It's going to take a while to explain all this to the others.'

'Have a bit of bait first,' said Harris generously, handing over the bag. 'It's jolly good stuff. Very moreish. I can't think why the fish don't like it.'

Thursday looked across at Harris's line floating limply on the water. 'I thought they did,' he said. 'The bit you put in just now seems to have gone, anyway.'

'What!' wailed Harris, jumping to his feet. 'My bait – *gone*! Of all the . . .'

'See you later,' called Thursday.

But Harris was much too busy pulling in his line to reply. The hook seemed to have got itself tangled with some weed near the bank. And, as he made his way across the fields, Thursday could hear snatches of a voice raised in anger as it addressed itself to the stream in general and its inhabitants in particular.

'Parasites . . .

'Living off other people's bait . . .

'I'll catch you one day . . .

'I'll make you laugh on the other side of your gills . . .

'Just you wait . . . I'll catch you. . .'

Gradually, as he drew near to the church, the sound died away and Thursday turned his thoughts to the more important matter of how he was going to explain the whole affair to the rest of the Cupboardosities.

As he entered the church and began the long climb

up to the organ loft cupboard his face grew longer and longer.

'My dear child,' exclaimed Mrs Peck, catching sight of him as he poked his head through the hole in the floor. 'What on earth's the matter?'

'Look as if you've just been to yer own funeral,' agreed Mr Peck. 'You've got a face as long as a rake. Come on, out with it. What's up?'

Thursday took a deep breath. 'Does anyone here like birds?' he inquired hopefully.

4   . . . And some Cogs begin to Turn

Uncle Ponty stared up at the huge, wooden shape looming in front of him and gulped.

'Of all the foolhardy ideas,' he exclaimed. 'It's as high as a lamp-post.'

'And twice as slippery, if you ask me,' said Mr Peck, examining the outside.

'And this bird,' asked Uncle Ponty, turning to Harris, 'you say it's imprisoned somewhere near the top?'

'Right at the very top,' replied Harris. 'You'll be able to see it later on when the door opens. At least,' he continued lamely, 'you would be able to if the light were on.'

'Ah . . . ah . . . ah . . . ahtishoo!' A bellow from somewhere near the window saved Harris from the remark which had already formed on Uncle Ponty's lips.

'Ssh!' said Uncle Ponty crossly, turning his wrath on the intruder. 'Don't make so much noise whoever you are.'

'It's all right,' replied a familiar voice. 'It's only me.'

'Huh! Trust you, Washin'ton,' grumbled Uncle Ponty, as the owner of the voice groped his way through the darkness towards them. 'I wonder you don't stand up at the window and tell the whole world we're here while you're about it.'

'I can't help it,' said Uncle Washington. 'Never did like birds. They make me sneeze.'

'Sneeze?' echoed Uncle Ponty. 'Don't see how a bird can make you want to sneeze.'

'Dust in the feathers,' explained Uncle Washington briefly. 'All right now. Got it out of me system.'

Uncle Ponty brushed himself down. 'It may be out of your system,' he said stiffly, 'but it's all over my coat. Worse than a fountain. I can't think why we came here in the first place.'

'Where's this contraption?' boomed Uncle Washington. 'Can't see a blessed thing. Didn't anyone bring a light?'

'It's right in front of your nose,' said Uncle Ponty. 'If you spent less time sneezing with it and more using it for what it was intended you wouldn't have to ask.'

Uncle Washington stood back and gaped. 'Don't tell me we've got to climb right up there!' he exclaimed.

Mr Peck groaned. 'Not another one! We've been all through that once. Where have Harris and Thursday got to?'

Putting his paw to his lips he gave vent to a loud whistle. Almost immediately a creaking sound broke out from somewhere overhead and a huge glass door swung open as Thursday jumped to the floor. 'It's all right everyone,' he exclaimed. 'We've got it open.

Harris brought a piece of wire and we used it as a lever.'

'By Jove,' said Uncle Washington admiringly. 'That was quick!' He clambered up onto a box and peered inside the opening with interest. 'Listen!'

Everyone in the room fell silent until the only sound left was the heavy breathing of Uncle Washington as he crawled through the open door in order to get a better view.

'Can't hear anything,' said Uncle Ponty at last.

'Neither can I,' exclaimed Uncle Washington.

'Well, why ask us to listen then?' grumbled Uncle Ponty. 'Never heard of anything so silly. Trying to hear something that isn't there.'

'That's just the point,' said Uncle Washington patiently. 'Harris said there was some machinery. If there's machinery why can't we hear it working?'

'Don't like it,' exclaimed Uncle Ponty. 'Don't like it at all.' He looked round uneasily. 'I've a nasty feeling in my bones. Machinery that works is bad enough, but machinery that isn't working is worse still. You never know when it's going to start up. It's probably some kind of fiendish Grumbly trick . . .'

Uncle Ponty broke off as a cry of pain came from somewhere inside the box. 'What's up?' he exclaimed in alarm. 'Have they got you?'

'There's a sort of round platform thing in here,' complained Uncle Washington in a muffled voice. 'I've just banged my head on it.'

51

'Is that all?' said Uncle Ponty, in a mixture of relief and disappointment. 'Thought something awful had happened.'

Thursday joined him inside the box. 'Harris says there's another one like it near the top,' he explained. 'They're both on chains and they both go up and down. Sometimes one side goes up – sometimes it's the other.'

'But never the two together, eh?' said Uncle Washington. 'Cunning – very cunning!'

'Reminds me of something,' said Uncle Ponty thoughtfully. 'Can't think what. Wish I could see a bit better.'

'Perhaps if one of us got up on the first platform,' said Harris, 'someone else could climb up the chain and jump across to the top one. Then he could lower some string down and pull the rest up.'

'Sounds a bit complicated,' said Uncle Washington doubtfully, 'but at least we could have a rest up there before the final assault.'

'Might have time for a snack as well,' said Uncle Ponty hopefully. 'I've brought some sandwiches.'

Uncle Washington seemed to be having some difficulty in controlling himself. 'Come on, Ponty,' he said at last. 'I'll give you a leg up.'

'Oh, no you don't,' exclaimed Uncle Ponty hastily.

'I'll go first if you like,' said Thursday eagerly. 'I'm good at climbing.'

'Capital!' exclaimed Uncle Ponty enthusiastically.

'We shall need some volunteers to form a pyramid so that you can get on to the first platform. Harris, you can stand by with the string. Washington, you're long and thin, you'd better go after Thursday and pull the rest of us up. If you like to stand on my shoulders I'll give you a bunk up.'

Uncle Washington listened to the conversation with growing disfavour. 'And what,' he inquired suspiciously, 'will you be doing while all this is going on?'

'Bringin' up the rear,' replied Uncle Ponty promptly. 'Must have someone to bring up the rear.'

'Either you come with me,' said Uncle Washington firmly, 'or I don't go at all.'

'Blimey!' exclaimed Mr Peck. 'If you two argue about it much longer you'll be the only ones left. Half the family are up there already.'

'Good gracious!' exclaimed Uncle Washington in surprise. 'So they are!'

As he gazed up at the crowd of Cupboardosities, some still swarming up the chain, others clinging to the platform high above their heads, a cunning gleam came into his eyes. 'Excuse me, Ponty,' he said. 'I think one of your laces has come undone.'

Before Uncle Ponty had time even to say thank you, Uncle Washington bent down, grasped Uncle Ponty's back legs, and gave a tremendous heave.

Taken completely unawares, Uncle Ponty rocketed up into the air and just managed to save himself by grabbing hold of the edge of the bottom platform.

'You bounder, Washin'ton!' he roared. 'Of all the rotten, dirty tricks ... I've a good mind to ...' His voice broke off and then a note of alarm suddenly crept into it.

'Steady on, Washin'ton,' he called. 'The platform's movin' up.'

'Nonsense,' puffed Uncle Washington. 'It can't be.'

'I tell you it is,' gasped Uncle Ponty. 'Either that or I'm movin' down.'

Uncle Ponty's normally plump frame appeared to be stretched to its limit and there was quite a wide gap between his yellow waistcoat and the top of his trousers as he clung desperately to the slippery edge of the platform above his head.

'I reckon there's too much weight on the other platform,' said Mr Peck. 'Hold on – I'll get some of the others down.'

'What's the matter, Washin'ton?' called Uncle Ponty. 'What's goin' on down there? Get a move on. I can't hold on much longer.'

'I ... I ...' began Uncle Washington.

'What's that?' gasped Uncle Ponty. 'Can't hear. Hurry up, Washin'ton, for goodness' sake. I'm slippin' ...'

'I think I'm going to ... ah ... ah ... ahtishooooo!' The rest of Uncle Washington's words were lost as a tremendous roaring sneeze blasted and shook the inside of the case.

Before the astonished gaze of those who were still

54

outside waiting their turn up the chain Uncle Washington released his grasp of Uncle Ponty's legs and toppled over backwards.

As he let go a strange whirring noise broke out from somewhere overhead, followed almost at once by a steady rhythmic ticking, and the platform carrying Uncle Ponty suddenly rose into the air and disappeared from view.

At the same time the platform carrying Thursday and those members of the family who had already joined him came shooting down only to pull up suddenly near the bottom, spilling its occupants into a pile on the floor.

For a moment all was confusion as shouts and cries for help filled the air and then, before any of the Cupboardosities had time to gather their wits, another even more frightening event took place.

Somewhere in the distance there was the sound of a door being slammed, and for the second time that evening Mr Peck's whistle pierced the air, bringing some kind of order out of the chaos which reigned.

'Quick!' he shouted. 'Everyone hide. Look lively! It's the Grumblies!'

At the sound of the dreaded word fresh cries of alarm broke out from all directions and Thursday felt himself being lifted bodily off the ground as, with one accord, everyone made a wild dash for safety.

They weren't a second too soon for just as the last member of the Peck family found a hiding-place, the door opened and the room was flooded with light. But by then only the faintest movement of the curtains and the smallest rise and fall of the carpet betrayed the fact that anything was amiss.

The biggest rise and fall came from a small patch of carpet near the fireplace, where Thursday and Uncle Washington were sharing a hiding-place.

'By Jove,' whispered Uncle Washington, breathing heavily. 'That was a close shave.'

All over the room eyes peered out and watched unblinkingly as two figures entered the room, paused for a moment near the doorway, and then crossed to where a large clock stood against one of the walls, its glass door ajar.

Holding his breath until he felt as if he was about to burst, Thursday watched in silent fascination as the leading Grumbly gave a cry of disgust at the mess of string and cheese on the floor and then reached inside the clock-case and did something to the mechanism.

Almost immediately the whirring noise, which had been going on all the time in the background, suddenly reached a climax and as it did so a small door at the top of the clock swung open.

A hiss of indrawn breath went round the room as the figure of a bird emerged from the darkness within, leant over the end, and uttered a loud cuckoo-like cry.

But it wasn't the bird or its call which caused the watchers far below to gasp with alarm. As a bird, in fact, it was slightly disappointing. From Harris's

somewhat vivid description most of those present had prepared themselves for something in the nature of a large golden eagle with huge talons and a beak the size of a Grumbly's scythe; whereas the creature which hung poised above their heads was small and rather moth-eaten.

The sight which struck a chill to the hearts of the watchers on the floor was that of the familiar figure of Uncle Ponty clinging helplessly to the bird's back as it swayed to and fro above their heads.

Three times the door opened. Three times the bird appeared, and three times Uncle Ponty's cry for help rose high above its call.

'See that?' breathed Uncle Washington. 'Poor old Ponty!'

From their various hiding-places the Cupboardosities watched with bated breath as the first Grumbly gave a cry of surprise and, when the door opened for the fourth time, reached up and caught Uncle Ponty in his hand, holding him up for the other to see.

At first it looked as if he was going to toss Uncle Ponty through the window into the night, but then, after some kind of an argument he appeared to change his mind and instead wrapped him in a handkerchief and carried him out of the room.

As the light went out and the voices died away, the Cupboardosities came out of their hiding-places one by one and assembled in a group in the middle of the room eyeing each other with consternation.

'A bloomin' cuckoo clock!' exclaimed Mr Peck in disgust.

'Not even a real bird,' exclaimed Uncle Washington. 'A blessed stuffed one!'

'Where's that Harris?' asked Mr Peck.

'That's right, where is he?' repeated Uncle Washington. 'It's all his fault.'

'Voles,' said Mr Peck bitterly as he looked round the room. 'They're all the same them voles. Can't see beyond the ends of their noses. About time he bought himself some glasses.'

But Harris had disappeared. Wisely he was either still in hiding or else he had taken advantage of the confusion and gone off home. Either way he was no-where to be seen.

'The long and the short of it is,' said Mr Peck soberly, bringing everyone back to earth with a bump, 'old Ponty's a prisoner now, so what are we going to do about it?'

'I didn't like the look on that Grumbly's face,' said Uncle Washington ominously. 'Didn't like it at all. Don't think he took to old Ponty, either. If you ask me he's got something nasty in mind.'

At Uncle Washington's words a shiver went round the room.

'So long as it stays in his mind,' said Mr Peck, pulling his coat collar up, 'we're all right. It's when it comes out the trouble's going to start.'

Uncle Washington nodded. 'Poor old Ponty,' he said grimly. 'I wouldn't like to be in his shoes when that happens. Not for all the cheese in France.'

5 The Rescuing of Uncle Ponty

The Cupboardosities were holding a council of war. All the family, with one notable exception, were present. The exception was Uncle Ponty, who was also the subject under discussion.

There was a general air of gloom about the proceedings and very wisely Thursday was keeping quietly in the background. Although no one had actually blamed him for his part in the previous night's disaster, Harris's name had come up several times in the course of conversation and Uncle Washington in particular had passed one or two very pointed remarks.

'I'm sorry, my dear,' he said, pushing aside a plate of home-made cream cheese as he turned to Mrs Peck. 'Can't touch it tonight, I'm afraid. The thought of poor old Ponty – a prisoner of the Grumblies – makes it stick in me throat.'

'I should try and eat something,' replied Mrs Peck. 'We shall need all our strength if we're going to rescue him.'

'Quite right, Ma.' Mr Peck, whose appetite was second only to Uncle Ponty's, dipped his paw into the mound as it went past. 'No use crying over spilt milk. Must keep our peckers up.'

'Rescue him!' repeated Uncle Washington. 'We

don't even know where he is. I've looked everywhere and I can't find him. He might just as well have disappeared off the face of the earth. Birds! If anyone mentions that word to me again . . .'

Uncle Washington broke off half-way through the sentence but he left his listeners in no doubt as to his feelings on the matter.

Unnoticed by the others, Thursday slipped sadly from the room and made his way out of the church, across the field, and over the bridge in the direction of Harris's hut by the stream.

Somehow life without Uncle Ponty had lost much of its savour. Despite his continual arguments with Uncle Washington, or perhaps even because of them, Uncle Ponty was as much a part of the Pecks' home as the oak floorboards of the organ loft cupboard itself. The thought of his being kept a prisoner for the rest of his life, or perhaps suffering an even worse fate, filled Thursday with dismay.

Usually on a summer's evening Harris was to be found sitting outside his tin hut day-dreaming, or fishing, or even both at the same time, for the two went well together. But, to his great surprise, when he reached the river-bank, Thursday found it deserted.

He knocked on the side of the hut and called out several times, but all to no avail. He was about to leave when there was a crashing in the nearby undergrowth and seconds later a familiar figure, red in the face and

61

very much out of breath, burst through a patch of heather and collapsed at his feet.

'I ... *phew* ... I ... *phew* ... I *phew*.' Harris sounded for all the world like some ancient railway engine condemned to spend the rest of its days shunting to and fro on a siding.

Thursday waited patiently for a while and then scooped up some water with his paw. 'Here, have a drink,' he said, holding it out to his friend.

'Thanks ... *phew*. Glad I found you ... *phew*. Thought you might be here.' Harris sat on the bank fanning himself with his straw hat, his chest heaving in and out while he gathered his breath. 'To cut a long story *phew* ... short,' he said at last, 'I've found him!'

'You've *what*!' Thursday jumped to his feet and gazed at Harris with unconcealed admiration. 'Uncle Ponty? You've found him! Where?'

'In a shed in a cage at the back of the Grumblies' house.'

'In a shed in a cage?' repeated Thursday.

'I mean – in a cage in a shed,' said Harris. '*Phew!* You've no idea how I've been running.'

'Is he . . . ?' Thursday sought for words to express what was in his mind.

'He's alive, if that's what you want to know,' said Harris simply. 'At least, he was when I left him because he was snoring. Unless they were groans,' he exclaimed, sitting up suddenly. 'I hadn't thought of that. No, I don't think they were. They were definitely snores.'

'We'd better tell the others,' said Thursday, getting up to go.

'Wait for me,' exclaimed Harris. 'I'll just get my fishing-rods.'

'You remember that cuckoo clock?' he continued. 'Well, this cage where they're keeping Uncle Ponty a prisoner is even worse. It's hanging on a chain from the roof. There's no way up at all.

'I thought if we do nothing else we could at least get some food up to him on the end of a line.' Harris paused in the doorway to his hut. 'I say, you won't forget to mention that *I* found him will you?'

But Thursday was hardly listening. Instead he was

hurrying homewards as fast as his legs would carry him.

'Hey! Wait for me!' Harris dived into his hut, gathered several of his best rods, and a moment later followed hard on the heels of his friend.

Gradually, however, Harris's pace slowed down. He was still smarting over his mistake with the cuckoo clock and he began to feel that it mightn't be a bad idea if Thursday paved the way for him, as it were, with the news of his discovery.

Soon his run became a walk, then the walk turned into a dawdle, and long before he reached the church of St Mary's in the Valley the first of several long wailing blasts began sounding their warning note. They came from the direction of the organ loft and they echoed eerily again and again through the gathering dusk in the churchyard as Grandpa Aristide applied himself with unusual vigour to his conch-shell.

Somewhere in the distance a dog howled and Harris, rather wishing that he'd kept up with Thursday after all, took a firmer grasp of his rods as gradually, from many directions, there came the soft padding of feet and the gentle swaying of grass and undergrowth.

For a while there was a lull in the proceedings, then a ragged cheer broke out and shortly afterwards another movement spread out from the walls of the church. Unlike the first it was organized and purposeful, as of a small but determined army on the move. Certain creatures who had paused in their nightly stroll in order to investigate the strange goings on, quickly changed their minds and scattered to let it pass as it made its way down the hill towards the road and the distant glimmer of light from the house where Uncle Ponty lay prisoner.

Led by Mr Peck, the army began to swell in size as more and more passers-by joined the ranks, until, by the time it reached its destination, it seemed to stretch as far as the eye could see.

'Careful with that fishin'-rod,' growled Uncle Washington as Mr Peck brought them to a halt and Harris pushed his way to the front. 'Nearly had my eye out then.'

'Blow your eye,' said Mr Peck. 'Where's Ponty?'

In answer Harris pointed upwards towards the roof of the shed where a small cage, enclosed on three sides by wood and on the fourth by steel bars, swung lazily in the draught from an open window.

'The blighters!' exclaimed Uncle Washington. 'They don't mean him to escape. There's a five-foot drop at the very least.'

'I think I can hear something,' said Thursday.

Mr Peck held up his paw for silence. 'Listen.'

In the silence which followed, a steady rhythmic breathing, close to being a snore, came from the cage high above their heads.

'He's still alive, anyway,' said Uncle Washington.

He stood back and cupped his paws to his mouth. 'Hulloooo,' he called. 'Are you all right up there?'

Uncle Washington's shout was greeted by a series of grunts and snorts, followed by a smacking of lips and a faint rustle of straw as something stirred inside the cage.

'Who's there?' called a voice at last.

'It's us,' shouted Mr Peck. 'The family. We're all here.'

'Harris found you, Uncle Ponty,' cried Thursday, anxious to help his friend as much as possible. 'Now we've come to rescue you.'

For a moment there was silence and then a low groan echoed across the roof of the shed.

'Ponty!' cried Uncle Washington.

At the sound of Uncle Washington's voice the groan grew in volume and became so bloodcurdling it caused the watchers down below to start back in horror.

'Are you . . . are you all right?' cried Uncle Washington in alarm. 'They haven't been . . . I mean . . .'

'Save yourselves,' called Uncle Ponty weakly. 'Don't worry about me. I . . . I'll be all right. I . . . I've got my treadmill . . . the time passes. Leave me here and escape before it's too late . . .' His voice broke and a quiet sob came from somewhere inside the cage.

'By golly. Did you hear that?' Uncle Washington removed his hat and stood for a moment with his head bowed in silent reverence. 'I take back all I've ever said about old Ponty,' he continued. 'Selfish? That's one of the most unselfish things I've ever heard.'

'That settles it,' said Mr Peck briskly. 'We'd better do something – and quickly. Someone find a piece of cloth – any old piece will do. If we all get round in a circle and hold it, at least we'll break his fall.'

'We'd better try and get some food up to him first,' said Washington. 'He'll need some energy.'

'Not too much,' warned Mr Peck. 'You know old Ponty – we don't want him stuffing himself so much he gets stuck in them bars.'

'I've brought some bread,' said Thursday. 'Harris could get some up to him on one of his fishing-lines.'

Uncle Washington clapped his paws. 'Good man. All right, Ponty,' he called. 'Don't worry. Hang on. We're gettin' some grub up to you. Shan't be a moment.'

Any reply that Uncle Ponty might have made was lost in the general scuffling as the mice went about their tasks. A small group, led by Mr Peck, went in search of some cloth while Uncle Washington, Harris and Thursday busied themselves with the rod, line and bread.

When everything was ready, Harris lifted his rod and everyone waited patiently as he cast it in the direction of Uncle Ponty's prison.

'Good man,' said Uncle Washington, as Harris, after several unsuccessful attempts, at last managed to drop the hook over the edge of the cage and through the bars. 'Can you pull it in again?'

Harris began to grow red in the face as he turned his reel. 'I'm trying to,' he puffed, 'but I think it's jammed somewhere.'

Even as he spoke the line shifted slightly and almost immediately there came a soft plop, plop, plop on the floor of the shed.

'Good heavens!' exclaimed Uncle Washington, pointing a trembling paw towards an ever-widening pool of red by his feet. 'Blood!'

'Blimey!!' said Mr Peck. 'You must have caught the hook in old Ponty!'

'Don't think so,' gasped Harris. 'It feels more like

68

the bars or something.' He gave another tremendous heave and as he did so a shower of small objects suddenly pattered on the floor like rain.

Uncle Washington bent down to take a closer look. 'What on earth?' He dipped his paw into the pool of red by his feet, peered at it for a moment, and then gingerly applied it to his lips. 'Scoundrel!' he cried suddenly. 'Charlatan!'

'Blimey! What's the matter?' asked Mr Peck.

'Look!' Uncle Washington pointed a trembling paw at the floor. 'Blood indeed! That's not blood – that's tomato sauce!'

Mr Peck bent down and peered at the cause of Uncle Washington's wrath. 'There's a piece of *pâté* here, too,' he exclaimed with interest.

'And some cheese,' said Harris. 'Danish Blue!'

'Look at this,' cried Thursday, holding up a half-eaten piece of cake. 'Chocolate and Walnut!'

'Give me that line,' exclaimed Uncle Washington. 'There'll be some blood if he's not down here in five seconds – there'll be blood everywhere!'

'Hold on!' Uncle Ponty's voice high above their heads had a note of panic in it. 'I think I can hear someone coming. You'd better run for it. Hurry!'

'You'll hear someone coming in a minute all right,' spluttered Uncle Washington. 'It'll be me. *Starving indeed!* Living on the fat of the land! SAVE YOURSELVES! Leave you so that you can lie there gorging yourself more like it! Wretched deceiver!

Rogue! Knave! Swindler! Snake in the grass! Pecksniff!'

Uncle Washington's face changed rapidly from pink through various shades of red into a deep and ominous-looking purple. As it did so a door in the cage suddenly opened and a sheepish face peered down at them.

'I say,' said Uncle Ponty, reaching for Harris's line, 'are you annoyed about something, Washin'ton?'

As Uncle Washington's face rapidly turned an even deeper shade of purple Mr Peck held up a paw and, turning to the others, gave a broad wink. 'No sense in staying here if we're not wanted,' he said. 'May as well leave him. Shouldn't be surprised if they aren't fattening him up for something.'

'Mouse pie, very likely,' growled Uncle Washington. 'Serve him right.'

There was a whirr and a swish as Uncle Ponty slid down the line and landed by their side.

'You might have told me there was a hook on the end,' he grumbled. 'It could have torn my tongue out by the roots.'

'It didn't,' said Mr Peck.

'Or even pulled it to shreds.'

'It's still in one piece by the sound of it,' said Uncle Washington.

Uncle Ponty stuck out his tongue and squinted down his nose as he tried to view the end. 'Looks a bit red to me,' he said plaintively.

'Shouldn't wag it quite so much,' replied Uncle Washington unsympathetically. 'If you'd only give it a rest it might get better.'

Uncle Ponty turned and glared at the others. 'It would be nice,' he said stiffly, 'if I had a *bit* of sympathy. It's not very pleasant being a prisoner of the Grumblies I can tell you.'

'It would be even nicer,' replied Uncle Washington, 'if we had some thanks for rescuing you. Wish we'd left you now.'

'If it hadn't been for Harris you might still be there,' said Thursday, speaking up for his friend.

'Three cheers for Harris,' cried Uncle Washington.

A ragged cheer broke out from the ranks behind him. It was taken up first by one mouse and then another until in the end even Uncle Ponty joined in. But Harris had a faraway look in his eyes as he wound in his line and not even the combined cheers of the Cupboardosities and all the other mice who'd joined in Uncle Ponty's rescue appeared to have any effect.

'I think he's got his mind on other things,' explained Thursday. 'It's the first time he's ever made a catch, let alone landed one.'

6

In which Thursday makes a Wish and an Unexpected Visitor brings Food for Thought

'I wish,' said Thursday, one evening towards winter, 'I wish I could have another adventure.'

Harris gave a hollow laugh. 'You don't wish for things like that,' he said, dismissing the idea with a wave of his paw. 'Adventures happen. You mark my words, you'll meet one some time when you least expect it and then crash! bang! wallapoo! – you'll wonder what hit you.'

Thursday gave a sigh as he bade his friend goodbye and hurried off to work.

All in all it had been a busy summer, with little time left at the end of the day for thoughts of pleasure.

Together with the other Cupboardosities he'd spent much of his time out of doors gathering in the harvest of fruit. Early on there had been strawberries to pick, then had come the cherries, and later still, towards autumn, delicious nuts and blackberries.

Suddenly, however, it had grown colder. And with the change in the weather, and the hard work of summer behind him, Thursday had begun to grow restless.

In the circumstances Harris's words were cold comfort, but unknown to either of them they were to come true sooner than expected.

It all began with the arrival a few days later of a postcard bearing a most unusual stamp. The card was labelled CIVIC CENTRE, MOUSEVILLE, TENNESSEE, and showed a picture of a large building which seemed to reach up and up like a long stone finger until it almost touched the sky.

Thursday had never seen such a tall building before and he examined the card with interest while the rest of the family discussed the matter.

On the reverse side, apart from the address, were the hastily written words ARRIVING OLD COUNTRY ANY MOMENT. IF NOT SOONER. WATCH OUT. WHAM! H.P.C. JNR.

'I've looked for the word "wham" in a dictionary,' said Uncle Washington, 'and it doesn't seem to mention it, but I've found Mouseville, Tennessee, on a globe and it's in America.'

'America!' Mr Peck scratched his head. 'Don't know as we've got any friends in America have we, Ma?' he asked.

'Corncrake!' Grandpa Aristide spun the wheels of his chair and pushed his way to the front. 'Your Grandmother's sister married a Corncrake just after the war,' he said, addressing Mrs Peck. 'He came over in a troopship and then took her back to America to live.'

'So she did,' exclaimed Mr Peck. 'All comes back to me now. One of the G.I. Brides she was.'

'No one ever saw her again,' continued Grandpa Aristide, 'but by all accounts she did very well for herself.'

'Well, I never.' Mrs Peck began to look most excited. 'I remember Grandad telling me all about Uncle Otis Corncrake – that must have been their son.'

'And he had a son called Howard,' said Grandpa Aristide. 'I've got a picture of him in me album. Fine lad.'

'So H.P.C. JNR must stand for Howard P. Corncrake, junior,' said Uncle Washington. 'And Bob's your uncle.'

'Bob?' echoed Uncle Ponty, looking up from a bowl of condensed milk. 'Thought you said his name was Howard.'

Uncle Washington sighed. 'If you spent less time stuffin' yourself,' he began, 'and more time listenin'...'

'And if you folks want to know what the P stands for, it stands for Progress, progress with a capital P.'

Thursday, who'd been sitting with his back towards the door idly sharpening a piece of wood, jumped more than anyone as an unfamiliar voice with a strange accent broke across the conversation.

He turned to find himself staring up at a tall stranger in an enormous wide brimmed hat, a pair of dark glasses, a number of mysterious-looking leather cases slung on straps round his neck, and a shirt of such an astonishing variety of colours it caused him to blink in amazement.

'Gee, I'm sorry if I startled you.' The stranger looked most upset at the surprise he'd caused. 'Howard P. Corncrake,' he announced, raising his hat and bowing low. 'At your service. Hi, everybody!'

'Hi!' echoed the Cupboardosities doubtfully.

'We didn't expect you quite so soon, Howard,' said Mrs Peck, recovering from her confusion. 'We've only just got your card. I thought it would be at least another week or two.'

Howard began loosening some of his straps. 'I hopped on an airliner!' he said carelessly.

'An *airliner*!' exclaimed Thursday. 'I've been up in a balloon, but I've never been up in an aeroplane.'

'Breakfast in New York, lunch in England. I tell you, it's the only way to travel,' said Howard. 'The guys at the airport back home, they got the whole thing buttoned up. For two dollars ninety you get the Executive Suite in one of the wings.'

Howard paused for breath and glanced across the room as Grandpa Aristide gave a loud sniff. 'Guess I smell a bit of gasolene,' he said apologetically, 'but for two dollars ninety who's complaining? I got a bed – reclining seats – first-class service. I tell you, for me travelling by sea is out from now on.'

'You must be hungry after your long journey,' said Mrs Peck, bustling around to make room for their unexpected guest. 'Sit down and I'll get you something to eat.'

'Not for me, Aunt Peck,' said Howard. 'I had the works. Soup . . . Chicken Maryland . . . Ice Cream with pistachio nuts and chocolate sauce . . . Caviare . . .'

Uncle Ponty listened to Howard's recital of his menu with an open mouth. 'I say,' he exclaimed, unable to contain himself any longer, 'can *anyone* go on one of these trips?'

'If you know the right people,' replied Howard, clicking his paws. 'You gotta know the right people, Unc. I gotta great trip lined up. London, England.

Paris, Italy. Rome, France. Or was it Paris, France. Rome, Italy? I don't know ... I'll have to look up my brochure ... I get kinda confused with all this travelling.'

As Howard flipped through a wad of papers and reeled off the list of all the places he intended visiting, the world suddenly seemed to shrink in size, and the Peck family fell silent as they listened in awe.

'Oh, dear,' said Mrs Peck, when Howard at last came to the end of his itinerary. 'I was going to suggest that if you're staying long you might like to look round our shop, but it must sound rather dull after all those exciting places.'

'Gee, Aunt Peck, there's nothing I'd like better,' exclaimed Howard. 'I have instructions from the folks back home that I gotta see everything and report back. They get kinda homesick at times for news of the old country.'

'Thursday can show you round this evening then,' said Mrs Peck. 'It'll be a nice treat for him. What do you think, Dad?'

'Good idea, Ma,' said Mr Peck warmly. 'I reckon he's earned a rest.'

'*Thursday!*' Howard looked most impressed. 'Gee, that's some name. Mind if I call you Thurs.?'

'Not at all,' said Thursday politely.

'Great,' said Howard, holding out his paw. 'Hiya, Thurs.'

'Er ... Hiya, Howard,' replied Thursday.

Howard pumped Thursday's arm up and down several times and then sat down in an arm-chair and removed his sun-glasses.

'Gee, this is some place you have here,' he exclaimed, surveying the room. 'I guess it's what we'd call "open plan" back home.'

'It's certainly open,' said Mrs Peck doubtfully, 'but I'm not sure that it was ever planned that way.'

'Kinda medieval, if you'll pardon the expression,' said Howard.

Mr Peck slapped one of the beams above his head. 'English h'oak. Four hundred years old and still as good as new.'

'Tradition,' said Howard. 'That's what I like to see – tradition. Back home we got a little shack in the country. Nothing much. You know – the usual – six up and six down and a swimming-pool, but nothing like this . . .'

'Wait until you see the shop, Howard,' said Thursday eagerly, amid a chorus of agreement from the other Cupboardosities. 'That's really old. Older than this organ loft cupboard even.'

A long, low whistle escaped from Howard's lips. 'This I gotta see, Thurs.,' he exclaimed. 'This I gotta see.'

'Good,' said Mrs Peck nervously. 'That's all settled then. Now you just sit there and rest while I make a cup of tea.'

Mrs Peck could feel a strangely unsettled air about

her family. It had been growing stronger and stronger ever since Howard's arrival and she had a nasty feeling about it in the back of her mind.

'I expect,' she said, 'you'll have lots of things to talk about.'

Howard nodded. 'I gotta million, Aunt Peck,' he said fervently. 'I gotta million.'

Howard was as good as his word, and if there weren't exactly a million things to talk about, at least there were many hundreds. It was late that night before roll-call was over and they at last set out for the shop.

Roll-call was a nightly affair in the household and always took place before the working-party left for Mr Peck's Exchange and Mart. With so many heads to count no one wanted to run the risk of missing one out or, worse still, counting the same one twice.

It was all much more complicated than it looked and sometimes took a very long time indeed.

Some of the older girls in particular caused a great many difficulties. Most of them took it in turns to stay at home and help with the housework, but one or two, led by Desdemona, who didn't like soiling her paws, went to great lengths to avoid doing any such thing.

To make matters worse Ethel, who'd once had a nasty experience in the dark and was very nervous in consequence, sometimes dug her heels in and refused to go out for weeks on end, so that Mr Peck was kept very busy making sure everyone did their fair share of work.

Each night, after roll-call, the Cupboardosities took a different route to the shop, forming a long line and holding on to each other's tails as they made their way down the alleys and lanes worked out the day before.

In this way they kept safe from sudden attacks by cats and other nasty creatures who might be lying in wait for them. But for once the rules were relaxed in honour of their visitor and Thursday was allowed to walk in front with Howard by his side so that he could point out the various sights of interest on the way.

Mr Peck's Exchange and Mart Grocery Store was not the sort of shop one would normally notice from the outside. It was very close to the ground and during the daytime the shutters were kept tightly closed so that it was quite easy to mistake it for a simple ventilator grill in the wall and pass it by.

The only sign that there was anything out of the ordinary came from a strong smell of cheese and a small faded notice above the shutter which said MR PECK'S EXCHANGE AND MART DELICATESSEN. ESTABLISHED A VERY LONG TIME AGO.

But once inside the door, things were very different. The shop itself was one vast high-ceilinged room with spotlessly clean whitewashed walls and a floor which was neatly covered with a layer of freshly brushed sawdust. Several rows of candles cast a warm glow over the food-laden counters lining the four walls, and in the centre of the room, on a raised platform, stood the desk where Mr Peck sat and supervised the operations.

Thursday felt very important as he led Howard down the length of the room and pointed out the various counters.

Just inside the door there was a special one for cooked meats of all description. Ham, pork, beef – both corned and roast – *pâté* and chicken, not to mention several kinds of liver sausage, English, Swiss, Belgian, French and German; for many of Mr Peck's customers were quite well-to-do and much of his stock was imported at great expense in order to titillate their palates.

The second counter was hardly less impressive for, apart from such humdrum things as pieces of potato, carrots – sliced and whole – onions, cabbage and lettuce, it also boasted a special section devoted to more exotic items such as mangoes, guavas, fresh pineapple, and other delicacies too numerous to be mentioned. This section in particular was very popular with some of the more affluent mice who lived on the hill on the other side of the village and did a lot of entertaining.

Next to it, by the far wall, a third counter groaned under the weight of biscuits, cakes and pastries and a thousand and one tit-bits cunningly arranged to tempt even the most jaded of appetites.

But it was the fourth counter which was Mr Peck's

pride and joy, for it ran the whole length of one wall, and on it he kept his magnificent and justly famous display of cheese.

To serve on Mr Peck's cheese counter was considered a great honour and was a job much sought after by the small Cupboardosities who were sometimes allowed the scrapings at the end of the day.

There was Gruyère from Switzerland, Parmesan and Gorgonzola from Italy, Blue-veined cheese from Denmark, big red balls of Edam from Holland, Camembert, Brie, Cream and Roquefort from France, and all kinds from England and Wales, Cheddar, Cheshire, Gloucester, Caerphilly, Stilton and Wensleydale; the list was almost endless.

There were so many in fact that Thursday was quite out of breath by the time he'd recited all their names and he paused for a moment in order that Howard might take it all in.

To his surprise the Peck's visitor stood by his side with an expression on his face, not so much of admiration, as of sheer disbelief.

'Is anything the matter?' asked Thursday anxiously.

'Grab me a chair, Thurs.,' said Howard. 'Grab me a chair. I've seen everything now.'

Thursday did as he was bidden and then stood back and eyed Howard with growing concern. 'Don't you like it?' he exclaimed.

'Like it?' Howard searched in vain for some way of

expressing himself. 'Why, it's out of this world, Thurs. It's out of this world. I read about things like this in story books and I've seen it on television, but I never dreamed I'd see it for real.'

Thursday looked even more puzzled. 'Don't you have any shops in America?' he asked.

Howard slapped his knee. 'That's a laugh!' he exclaimed. 'That sure is a laugh. I gotta hand it to you, Thurs. You gotta sense of humour. Oh, boy!

'You know what gets me?' he continued. 'All you people working. The whole family. It's like something out of the Middle Ages. And all this unwrapped food! You know what this place would be back home?'

Thursday shook his head.

'Back home,' said Howard, 'this would be a Self Service Supermart. We did away with people slaving away behind the counters years ago. Back home we let the customers do the work. Result – we make more money!

'Do you know something? Back home we got cheese barons. Why, there's a guy called Al the Smell, he owns half the mouse cheese Supermarkets in New York alone. Does he work for a living? He just lies around all day by his swimming-pool, having his claws manicured. He don't even tap his own cigars out.

'And I'll tell you something else,' continued Howard, warming to his subject. 'We don't have

84

great lumps of cheese lying around the counters for all the customers to breathe over and touch – that's unhygienic. We have individually wrapped, pre-sliced, personalized, packaged cheese.'

Thursday began to feel more and more confused as he listened to the other. 'I don't think I've ever heard of that kind before,' he confessed.

'It's not a kind of *cheese*,' said Howard scornfully. 'It's a way of life. It means we cut it up into slices and wrap it in plastic. Take it or leave it – and boy, do they take it! I tell you, Thurs., we have a thing called the MCR – Mice Consumer Research – and they've studied these things. Why, we even have fleets of mobile cheese automats. Cheese cornets filled with the flavour of the month, all for the price of a nickel!'

Howard looked around Mr Peck's shop at the thronging mass of customers and at all the Cupboard-osities at work behind the counters and gave a long sigh. 'Boy,' he exclaimed. 'If I had my way you could all be millionaires in a month. Retired ones at that!'

'But it's always been like this,' said Thursday doubtfully.

'Is that any reason for not changing it?' inquired Howard scornfully. 'You gotta progress, Thurs. You just gotta progress.'

To that question neither Thursday nor even Mr Peck when the matter was put to him later, could find any satisfactory answer.

In fact, much later that night, when the shop was

closed and all the family were home and safely tucked in bed, Mr Peck lay awake long after the others had gone to sleep, and the longer he lay there the more difficult he found it to get to sleep himself.

'I don't know, Ma,' he said at long last, turning over and poking his wife. 'Perhaps he's right. Perhaps we *are* a bit behind the times.'

'Times are times,' replied Mrs Peck sleepily. 'I don't see how you can be in front of them, or behind them for that matter.'

Mrs Peck's words were small comfort to Mr Peck. In fact they added to his confusion and when he did finally get to sleep, it was only to dream of aeroplanes and of cheese and of a huge shop with his name written in neon lights on the walls outside – letters so tall that in reaching up to touch the top of them he fell out of bed and, on waking, found to his surprise that he was sitting on top of Thursday who was in the middle of a similar dream himself.

'You know what I think, Thursday?' he asked.

Thursday rubbed his eyes sleepily and shook his head.

'We gotta progress, Thurs.,' said Mr Peck. 'We just gotta progress.'

So saying Mr Peck climbed back into bed and lay with his paws crossed and a strange smile on his face.

'You've said a mouthful, Uncle Peck,' said a nasal voice from the other side of the room. 'You sure said a mouthful!'

7 Bad Business at Mr Peck's Exchange and Mart

Uncle Ponty stood in the middle of Mr Peck's shop and gazed around with growing astonishment.

In the short space of a few days a great change had come over everything. Counters, behind which generations of Pecks had served their apprenticeship to the grocery trade, had all been ripped out to make way for wire racks whose gleaming trays held mound upon mound of wrapped and packaged goods the like of which Uncle Ponty, for one, had never seen before.

The floor, swept clean of its sawdust, was so highly polished it shone like a freshly picked apple. The walls were powder blue, and overhead a loosely hanging sheet revealed traces of a ceiling which was now a delicate shade of pink. While from somewhere unseen, yet close at hand, a group of voices, soft and melodic, joined together in song for all the world like some heavenly choir.

Most significant of all, Mr Peck's platform and desk had been moved from its time-honoured position in the centre of the room to a place near the entrance alongside a row of baskets on wheels and a table laden with trays of small tit-bits.

'It's what I call THE PECKERY,' explained Mr Peck, pointing to the table. 'So as the customers can

'ave a sniff before they buys the goods so to speak. It's a
bit difficult when everything's already wrapped up.'

'Magnificent!' said Uncle Ponty, when at long last
he had taken it all in. 'Truly magnificent! Wouldn't
have believed it possible in the time.'

Uncle Washington, standing by his side, looked
most upset that someone else should have thought up
such a long word, let alone use it.

'Splendiferous!' he exclaimed, not to be outdone.
'That's the only word for it. Splendiferous!'

Uncle Ponty looked at his companion suspiciously.
'There's no such word,' he said petulantly.

'There is now,' replied Uncle Washington. 'I've just
invented it. An occasion like this demands a new
word.'

'Uncle Peck,' said Howard feelingly, 'I gotta hand
it to you. Boy, I gotta lump in my throat the size of a
corncob.'

'It's not bad,' said Mr Peck modestly. 'I reckon it'll
do for a start.'

'Not bad?' Howard's eyes gleamed behind his dark
glasses. 'Gee, that's good old British understatement.
If this doesn't bring the spondulicks rolling in nothin''
will. What are you going to do with all the loot, Unc.?
Buy a yacht? Two yachts? A castle?'

'Don't know as I've given it much thought,' said Mr
Peck, scratching his head. 'I've been too busy.'

'Boy, then you've got problems,' exclaimed
Howard. 'Because from now on you're going to be

loaded. That cash register's going to be playing a symphony and all the notes are going to be £, *s*. and *d*. Why, I can hear it now . . .' A dreamy expression came over Howard as he gazed upwards, an expression which was replaced almost immediately by one of puzzlement.

'Say,' he exclaimed, 'talking of music, what *is* going on? Can anyone hear what I can hear?'

'Oh, dear, in the excitement I almost forgot,' said Mrs Peck. 'It's our little surprise – Desdemona and the Angels.'

As she spoke Mrs Peck gave a sharp tug at a cord hanging from the ceiling and pulled away the sheet to reveal a large golden cage behind the bars of which could be seen a group of unusually clean-looking Cupboardosities, their paws crossed and their voices raised in unison.

Every now and then when they reached a high note, Desdemona appeared to be having trouble with her cardboard wings as they caught in the bars, and some of the smaller mice looked slightly apprehensive as the cage swung in time with the music, but the overall effect was so surprising, the watchers down below burst into a round of spontaneous applause.

'If this doesn't sell the idea, Unc., nothing will,' exclaimed Howard. 'This is genius. Sheer genius. Why, I can see it all. The crowds. The doors opening. The rush to get inside and then the choir. Everybody struck dumb as they wander round with their baskets.

Here Comes Thursday!

Picking up a piece of liver sausage here, a pack of cookies there. A morsel of cheese. Why, you can have music to suit what you want to sell. When you want to sell cheese you can have cheese music . . .'

'Cheese music?' chorused the others.

'*Cheese my lady love,*' explained Howard, breaking into song as he executed a tap dance in the middle of the floor. '*She is my doll, my baby dove.* Boy, I wish I didn't have to go on to Rome tomorrow night. This, I would like to see. They won't know what's hit 'em until they're back outside.'

'When are you going to open?' asked Uncle Washington. 'I must say I'd like to see it myself.'

'Tonight,' said Mr Peck. 'There's no time like the present. Just as soon as Thursday's finished the sign.'

Thursday, who during all the excitement had been sitting by himself in a corner with a large pot of white paint and a piece of wood, paused for a moment in his labours. 'I've almost finished,' he announced. 'I'm just tidying up. How many "P's" are there in "Super"?'

'One,' replied Uncle Washington. 'If you had two that would spell supper.'

'Supper?' Uncle Ponty appeared suddenly as if by magic from behind one of the wire racks. 'Did I hear someone say supper?'

Uncle Washington opened his mouth but before he had time to reply Mr Peck hastily interrupted him. 'Good idea,' he said. 'We're going to be busy tonight and I could do with a bite myself.'

'Excellent!' exclaimed Uncle Ponty, giving Uncle Washington a triumphant stare. 'Some of these goodies make my mouth water.'

'I'll put the sign outside,' said Thursday eagerly.

Mr Peck nodded. 'We'd better allow time for the word to get around,' he said.

'Hold it everyone,' called Howard, undoing one of his leather cases. 'I'm gonna take some pictures. This I gotta have for the record.'

Howard's words caused a flutter of excitement to run round the room and the cage above their heads swayed alarmingly as Desdemona and her Angels crowded to one side in the hope of being included in the photograph.

'Oh, dear, I feel as nervous as can be,' said Mrs Peck. 'I only hope we're doing the right thing.'

'Right or wrong,' replied Mr Peck, 'it's done now, Ma. It's what's known as progress.'

'I don't care what they call it,' said Mrs Peck. 'It doesn't make me like it any the more. One gets used to the old ways. I'm so worried we shall attract the wrong type of customer.'

Mr Peck avoided his wife's gaze. 'If everyone felt like that, Ma,' he said, 'there'd be nothing new in the world at all. 'Sides, it's not just us. We've got to think of the children.'

Mr Peck tried to sound enthusiastic but a note of sadness crept into his voice.

Mrs Peck looked at him anxiously. 'You don't think

we *have* done the wrong thing do you?' she asked.

Before Mr Peck had a chance to answer, Howard's voice suddenly rang out over the assembly.

'Can you hear what I can hear?' he cried. 'There's someone singing.'

'Desdemona ...' began Mrs Peck.

'No, not the Angels,' said Howard. 'Listen ... there's someone else. In fact, not just someone ... there's a whole army.'

'Good heavens!' exclaimed Uncle Washington as the room fell silent. 'You're right. What's that they're singing? "Why are we waiting?" '

'Must be hundreds of 'em,' said Uncle Ponty. 'Sound pretty impatient to me.'

Even as he spoke the door began to shake as someone gave it a hard thump on the other side and the noise was quickly taken up by others beating time to the tune the main body was singing.

'Why ... *thump* ... are ... *thump* ... we ... *thump* waiting ... *thump* ...'

'Quick,' shouted Mr Peck. 'Get rid of all these dirty things. Desdemona ... stand by with the music. Thursday ... hide that paint-pot somewhere.'

In a moment everything was in an uproar as the Cupboardosities hurried about their various tasks and then, almost as if by magic, the shop was suddenly once more spick and span.

'Aren't you goin' to perform the openin' ceremony?' asked Uncle Washington, as Mr Peck put on his apron and climbed up to the cash desk on the platform.

Mr Peck shook his head. 'I reckon Howard ought to do it,' he said. 'It's only right and proper. He gave us the idea in the first place.'

'Gee, Uncle Peck.' For once Howard looked quite taken aback. 'This sure is an honour. I just don't know what to say.'

'Don't say anything then,' said Uncle Ponty. 'Just open the door. If you don't they're liable to break it down by the sound of things.'

'You're right there,' said Howard, fumbling with the catch. 'You sure said a mouthful. Why, I remember . . .'

Whatever it was that Howard had been about to remember was lost for all time as the shutter slid up and a great tidal wave of shouting, struggling mice swept through the opening.

For a split second Howard rose above them and then, with one last despairing cry, he disappeared from view as the mass of bodies advanced into the shop and sucked him into their midst like some gigantic whirlpool. A whirlpool made up of shopping baskets, boxes, hats, coats, mice and yet more mice, mice almost without end. A whirlpool which screamed and fought and seemed to devour all before it, stripping the walls bare like an army of locusts, as it swept round the room.

How long it lasted no one knew. From their position

of safety on the platform, the Cupboardosities could only watch in horror. But it ended as suddenly as it had begun. One moment all was noise and confusion, the next moment the shop was empty and the only sound came from somewhere overhead, where Ethel was having hysterics in one corner of the cage while Desdemona fanned her with the end of a broken fan.

Mr Peck mopped his brow. 'Blimey! Is everyone all right?'

'No one missing?' asked Uncle Ponty, staggering to his feet.

'We'd better have another roll-call,' gasped Uncle Washington, 'just to make sure.'

'Howard!' exclaimed Mrs Peck suddenly, as a low moan came from somewhere near the door. 'What happened to Howard? He was right in their path.'

'Sounds as if he's chokin',' exclaimed Uncle Washington, rushing across the room. 'We'd better loosen his camera straps.'

The Cupboardosities crowded round Howard as he sat up rubbing his head. 'Gee, you ought to get that door fixed, Unc.,' he groaned. 'It's going to hurt someone real bad one day.'

'I think he must be delirious,' said Mrs Peck anxiously.

'Mean to say you don't remember what happened?' asked Mr Peck incredulously.

Howard looked puzzled. 'Remember? All I remember is opening the door and then ... wham!'

While he was speaking Howard looked around the room and as he did so his eyes opened wide. 'Jumping Jehozaphats!' he exclaimed. 'Have we been hit by a hurricane or something?'

'Might just as well have been for all that's left,' replied Mr Peck, gloomily surveying the bare room.

'I told you we would attract the wrong kind of customer,' sobbed Mrs Peck. 'I knew no good would come of it.'

'That's what I can't understand, Ma,' said Mr Peck. 'They *weren't* the wrong kind. They were the same ones as always. One or two hobbledehoys I must admit – but most of them were the usuals.'

'Recognized quite a few of the faces,' agreed Uncle Washington. 'Wouldn't say "boo" if you met 'em in the street, most of them. Must have been some sort of chain reaction. Once one started they all joined in.'

'If you ask me there's more in this than meets the eye,' said Uncle Ponty. 'By the look on their faces most of them didn't even expect to pay.'

Howard's face grew longer and longer as he listened to the Cupboardosities' tale of woe. 'Gee, Uncle Peck,' he said at last. 'I guess this is all my fault. I feel like a heel. A one hundred per cent heel.'

'Garn!' Mr Peck put his arm on Howard's shoulder as he tried to console him. 'Not your fault. Don't think it's anybody's fault. We weren't ready for it and neither were the customers. Tried to run before we could walk, that was our trouble. Fell over our own feet into the bargain. Should have done it gradual like.'

'Never mind,' said Mrs Peck. 'We'll start again. If we work hard . . .'

Mr Peck shook his head. 'It'll take more than hard work,' he said sadly. 'What with the winter coming on and Christmas just around the corner and everything . . . you can't sell things if you've nothing to sell. And you can't buy 'em in the first place if you've nothing to buy with. Can't even offer anything as a swop. It's all gone. It's going to be hard, Ma, I tell you that . . .'

'What's this? What's this? You're tired? Not surprised with all these goings on!' A familiar voice from the doorway caused everyone in the room almost to jump out of their skins with fright.

'Grandpa!' exclaimed Mrs Peck. 'What on earth are you doing here?'

'Thought I'd come down and see how you were getting on,' explained Grandpa Aristide, as he spun the wheels of his chair and entered the shop. 'Don't like it up there in the house all by myself with nothing to do and no one to talk to.'

'Blimey! You didn't come all the way down here on your tod, did you?' asked Mr Peck.

'What? Of course I did,' said Grandpa Aristide defiantly. 'No one else bothered to fetch me. Long time since I've been out. Quite enjoyed meself. Met a pair of mogs on the way but I gave 'em a couple of blasts on me conch-shell and they soon made off with their tails between their legs.'

Grandpa Aristide cackled at the thought and then peered round the shop at the upended piles of empty trays scattered about the floor. ' 'Pon me soul, I see you've made a success of this harebrained scheme after all. Take back all I said.'

'But, Grandpa . . .' began Mrs Peck.

Mr Peck laid a warning paw on her arm. 'It's all gone, Grandpa,' he said cheerfully. 'Not a bloomin' thing left in the shop.'

'What's that?' bellowed Grandpa Aristide. 'All gone? *Everything?* Don't tell me you haven't any pork dripping left!'

'Not a spot, Grandpa,' replied Mr Peck. 'Not enough to wet a fly's whistle even. The bowl's been scraped clean.'

Grandpa Aristide thumped the floor with his stick. 'How am I going to wax me whiskers then?' he cried. 'Tell me that! How am I going to wax me whiskers? I've always used best pork dripping and me father before me. What's the use of having a "Help Yourself Store" if you haven't got anything you can help yourself to?'

'Not "Help Yourself", Grandpa,' said Mrs Peck gently. ' "Self Service". That's quite a different thing.'

'That's not what is says outside,' growled Grandpa Aristide. 'Don't know your own business, that's your trouble. Now me whiskers are going to sag.'

Mr Peck exchanged a horrified glance with his wife and then joined the rush of Cupboardosities through the shop doorway and out into the street.

Thursday was one of the first outside. From his position in front of the crowd he looked up at the notice with a sinking heart, and as he read the words his knees began to tremble, for the board said, in large white letters:

GRAND OPENING

TONIGHT

FIRST TIME EVER

MR PECK'S

HELP YOURSELF SUPER MART

'Oh, Thursday,' said Mrs Peck, half in sorrow, half in anger. 'What *have* you done?'

'Gee, Thursday, I gotta hand it to you,' exclaimed Howard. 'When you do things you sure do 'em in a big way. I seen people dig holes for themselves before, but, oh boy, I never seen anyone dig one this deep before!'

8

The Rise and Fall of Harris

'We've got to do *something*.'

'We simply must.'

'Things can't go on like this.'

Thursday, pacing up and down the earthen floor of Harris's hut, his shadow becoming alternately large and small each time he passed the guttering night-light, counted off the points he was making on his paw.

Each point was punctuated by a cloud of steam as he paused for breath, for almost overnight winter had set in with a vengeance and the cold which had frozen hard the ground outside, turning every puddle into a sheet of ice, and covering every blade of grass with a sheath of white, penetrated even inside the hut.

Harris, sitting on his bed lost in thought as he listened to his friend, was hardly aware of the shivers which passed through his body every now and then. His boater and blazer had disappeared and had been replaced by a thick woollen scarf, but it was worn with an air of such gay abandon that its owner still managed to convey thoughts of warm summer evenings by the river.

'With the ground so hard,' continued Thursday, 'we can't dig for food, and with no money left we can't

buy any, and with nothing to sell we can't open the
shop, and with the shop closed we can't make any
money, so we're back where we started.'

'Where there's a will,' said Harris vaguely, 'there's
a way.'

'The trouble is,' said Thursday sadly, 'everyone
seems to have lost theirs. Ever since Howard left for
Rome Mr Peck just sits at home staring into space. It's
not like him at all. Even Grandpa Aristide is beginning to suspect something. It's no good, we must take
matters into our own paws. To start with . . .'

Harris looked up in surprise as his friend paused
by the nightlight with a worried look on his face. 'Is
anything the matter?' he asked.

'I've run out of claws,' said Thursday miserably. 'I can't make any more points. Everything's against us. We might just as well try flying to the moon.'

'What's that? What did you say?' Harris nearly fell off his bed with excitement. 'Say that again.'

Thursday thought for a moment. 'I only said everything is against us,' he exclaimed.

'No, not that,' said Harris impatiently. 'The other thing – about the moon.'

Thursday looked even more surprised. 'I only said we might just as well try flying to the moon – and so we might.'

To Thursday's surprise the words were hardly out of his mouth before Harris began dancing a jig up and down the middle of the floor, nearly blowing the light out in his excitement.

'Mind you don't set your scarf on fire,' he called.

Harris's only answer was to remove the offending article from his neck and wave it in the air above his head as he broke into renewed paroxysms of dancing.

'The moon! The moon!' he cried, as he whirled round in ever-decreasing circles, finally landing on his back beside Thursday with his feet up in the air and an expression on his face which suggested that all the world's problems were solved.

'I wish you'd tell me what it's all about,' said Thursday impatiently. Harris was subject to occasional fits of exuberance, which were all very well in their way, but they could also be somewhat annoying.

'It's simple,' replied Harris, suddenly becoming serious as he stood up and brushed himself. 'You know, of course, that the moon is made of cheese.'

Thursday nodded. 'Uncle Ponty always says it's best Gorgonzola.'

'Gorgonzola, Danish blue, Cheshire – it doesn't really matter,' said Harris. 'The fact of the matter is everyone agrees it must be made of cheese.'

'Uncle Washington doesn't,' said Thursday. 'He's read somewhere that it's made of dust. He's always arguing with Uncle Ponty.'

Harris looked put out for a moment and then he crossed the room and peered through a crack in the door. 'It's cheese,' he said. 'Definitely cheese. I can see it from here. Besides, if it was made of dust it would all blow away with the first wind. Right,' he continued, turning away from the door. 'What did you sell most of in your shop?'

'Cheese,' said Thursday promptly. 'Mr Peck specializes in cheese.'

Harris nodded. 'Exactly. Now, you want cheese in order to open up again and make a new start – right?'

'Right,' agreed Thursday.

'The moon is made of cheese,' said Harris. 'Right?'

'Er . . . right,' said Thursday doubtfully.

'In that case,' said Harris triumphantly, 'we'll go to the moon and get some.'

Thursday looked at his friend unbelievingly for a few seconds. 'Go to the moon?' he exclaimed at last. 'How can anyone possibly go to the moon?'

In the course of their short friendship Harris had come out with some wild schemes, but this seemed the wildest one of all.

Harris looked slightly put out. 'The Grumblies are trying to,' he said, as he began rummaging around on his bed, 'so I don't see why we shouldn't. They're building rockets. I've got a picture here somewhere in an old newspaper. If you want my opinion they're trying to steal a march on us. It's up to the mice of the world to unite. Why, just think of it – there must be enough cheese up there to last us for the rest of our lives. Mountains of it. Vast untapped sources.'

Harris stood up, red in the face, clasping a torn piece of paper in his paws. 'There!' he announced triumphantly. 'What did I tell you?'

Thursday took the piece of paper and studied it carefully. It showed what appeared to be a long upright silver sausage, pointed at the top end, with flames belching out from the bottom.

'That's a rocket,' explained Harris. 'And see what it says underneath. MOON LANDING IN OUR TIME – OFFICIAL!'

'I've seen one of those,' exclaimed Thursday excitedly.

'You have?' Some of Harris's enthusiasm began to melt like ice cream on a summer's day. 'Where?'

'Baron Munchen's,' said Thursday. 'I saw it only the other day when I was up there delivering groceries.'

'Baron Munchen's!' Harris shivered and gave vent to a rather sickly smile as he sat down on his bed. 'Don't you think we ought to leave it a day or two,' he remarked casually. 'There's no sense in rushing into these things . . .'

Thursday paused in the act of buttoning his coat. 'What's up?' he demanded. 'You're not scared, are you? It was your idea.'

'Scared?' Harris's voice sounded unusually high. He cleared his throat and tried again. 'No, of course not,' he repeated in a much deeper tone.

'Well, come on then,' exclaimed Thursday, winding his scarf tightly about his neck in order to keep out the cold. 'We've got no time to lose.' He gave a sniff as he stood in the doorway. 'I should wrap up. If you ask me, there's snow in the air.'

Harris followed shortly after his friend. By the look on his face he didn't much relish the idea of exchanging the comfort of his own home for the doubtful privilege of paying a visit to Baron Munchen's.

Baron Munchen lived alone in a gloomy old deserted house on a patch of heath outside the village, a house to which even the Grumblies gave a wide berth as they passed by.

The Baron always wore a black cloak over his shoulders, with a dark, wide-brimmed hat to match, and he had a reputation in the village for carrying out 'experiments'.

These rumours were borne out by the numerous bangs and puffs of smoke which issued from his house at regular intervals and many tales were told of the 'goings on' which took place in the dead of night.

To be threatened with being sent to Baron Munchen's as a punishment for misdeeds was considered to be a fate almost worse than death itself by the younger members of the neighbouring families.

'It's all right,' said Thursday, as they drew near. 'He's quite harmless when you get to know him. People just don't understand him, that's all.'

He led the way along an overgrown driveway to where a sign in the shape of a skull and crossbones with the words MUCH MUNCHEN – TRESPASSERS VERBOTEN, pointed the way towards a door in the side of the house.

'Perhaps he's not at home,' said Harris hopefully, as Thursday knocked for the second time.

'I think he is,' replied Thursday, nodding briefly skywards. 'I can see steam coming out of a grating up there.'

Harris looked up and then hastily lowered his eyes again. From close to, the Baron's house seemed even more eerie than ever. It rose up out of the tangled undergrowth and silhouetted itself against the sky, its

broken chimney-pots heeling over at a curious angle, looking for all the world like the gnarled fingers of some old witch.

At that moment the sound of a bolt being withdrawn, followed by the clanking of chains, came from somewhere inside and almost immediately the door was flung open to reveal the Baron himself standing in the gloom.

At the sight of Thursday his mouth opened in a slow smile. 'Ach! My young delicatessen friend, is it not?' he exclaimed, in an accent as thick as mulligatawny soup. 'And vot brings you here at such an hour?'

Quickly Thursday explained the purpose of their visit.

'A trip to the moon? Mein gootness!' Even the Baron seemed slightly taken aback at the magnitude of the request. 'Difficult things I can do at once, you understand? But the impossible, zis takes time!'

The Baron ushered them into his house, closed the door, and then led the way across the darkened hall and up a flight of linoleum-covered stairs.

'Why are his teeth all rusty?' whispered Harris.

'Ssh!' Thursday put his paw to his lips. 'That's not rust – that's gold!'

Beginning to feel impressed in spite of himself, Harris relapsed into silence only to cry out in alarm as they reached the first landing and something brushed across his face.

'Vebs,' said the Baron briefly. 'Spiders' vebs. I am working on a plan to collect zem for making Christmas stockings.

'So,' he continued, opening a door at the end of the passage. 'You vish to go to ze moon?'

Thursday looked round the Baron's workroom at all the various bits and pieces of apparatus which lined the walls. 'We haven't much time, that's the trouble,' he said.

The Baron nodded. 'Zis is ze truth. You know vy?'

Thursday and Harris shook their heads.

'Because,' said the Baron, glaring up at the sky through a hole in the roof, 'someone has been eating it! For some time I hov been keeping der close vatch and someone mit a large appetite has been stealing it piece by piece. Always, in time, the pieces are returned. But one day . . . Pfffft!' The Baron left his audience in no doubt as to what he thought would happen.

'You are in the vay of goot luck,' he continued, as he cleared a space on one of his benches, briskly sweeping aside a pile of old test-tubes, pieces of wire and other mysterious-looking objects. 'I hov a rocket vitch I made myself from some bits mit pieces I . . .'ow shall I say?' the Baron coughed somewhat guiltily, '*found* at the time of Guy Fawkes. A little extra gunpowder here – a little there– ya, I think a trip to the moon would be possible. But ve shall have to hurry.' He paused for a moment in order to peer through a near-by telescope made from a cardboard tube. 'See, approaching the storm clouds already are.'

'I'm ready,' said Thursday confidently.

'And your young friend, he is ready, too?' asked the Baron.

'Oh, yes, I think so,' exclaimed Harris, becoming eager in spite of himself.

'Goot!' The Baron rubbed his hands together. 'Then ve must vaste no time. Ve vill start immediately, if not before.'

'Immediately?' Harris's jaw dropped and even Thursday looked slightly surprised. 'Now! But we haven't even packed.'

'Packed!' mimicked the Baron. 'You hov not packed. Vot is zis you are going on? A holiday? You think on the moon your buckets mit spades you are needing? Psssshaw!'

Thursday and Harris exchanged uneasy glances as the Baron gave vent to a guttural snort and disappeared into a corner where he began busying himself with some bottles of chemicals and a pestle and mortar, the contents of which he eventually carried up a pair of steps and poured through a funnel into a large tubular object on the end of a stick which was standing in a jam-jar in the centre of the room.

After ramming the powder home with a long rod the Baron began lashing several crosspieces of wood to the main stem. 'Help I shall need mit zis,' he called, tossing down a length of string to Harris. 'Some fisher knots, I zink. You vill have to duck mit your heads ven I light ze fuse,' he explained, as Harris joined him on the precarious perch near the top. 'Otherwise your viskers may be singed.'

'You mean we have to go all the way to the moon hanging on to those bits of wood?' exclaimed Harris, peering shortsightedly up at the crossbars as the Baron passed him on the way down.

The Baron looked most offended. 'At such short notice you expect to travel first class?' he exclaimed. 'Poof! For two slices of apple strudel the whole project I would call off without even the count-down starting.'

'No, don't do that,' cried Thursday hastily, as the Baron made to put his matches away. 'We'll be all right.'

There were still a number of questions he would have liked to ask, not the least of which was how they were going to get back down to earth again after they'd reached the moon, particularly if they were heavily laden with cheese, but as he climbed the steps to join his friend, Thursday could already feel the Baron breathing heavily down his neck.

'Quick,' hissed the Baron, pushing him to one side as they reached the top. 'Burnt by the match I am being!'

Before Thursday had a chance to recover his balance the Baron leaned over and applied the flame to a piece of blue paper on the end of the rocket and then jumped back sucking his paw.

'Too late!' he cried, as Thursday climbed to his feet and tried to join Harris. 'Clear you must stand. The count-down ve are about to start. Ten . . . nine . . . eight . . .' Before the Baron had time to utter another word there was a tremendous flash and Thursday felt himself being hurled headlong into space.

For one brief second it felt as if the whole world had blown up around him as the explosion which followed rocked the room, and then gradually everything became quiet again.

He stood up shakily, brushing the dust and debris from his fur, and then blinked several times in order to accustom his eyes to the darkness. Nearby, the Baron struggled with the steps which appeared to have fallen on top of him. In the centre of the room stood the empty jam-jar, its sides blackened by the blast from the rocket.

'Harris!' cried Thursday in alarm. 'Where's Harris? What's happened to him?'

The Baron paused in his efforts to free himself and then pointed silently up through the hole in the roof to where some red, white and blue stars were bursting in the sky.

Thursday gazed for a moment in horror as one by one the stars went out. 'Harris!' he called again at the top of his voice. 'Harris!'

The Baron removed a section of the steps from

around his neck. 'My friend, calling is no use,' he said gravely. 'For such a distance a megaphone you need. Even if the sky he is still in.'

Thursday dragged his eyes away from the gaping hole in the roof and stared at the Baron as he took in the full meaning of his words. Then he turned and ran.

He ran down the stairs, out through the front door, along the path, through nettles and undergrowth, and all the way back home as fast as his legs would carry him.

Only then did he stop, collapsing on the floor of the organ loft, gasping out his story between great gulps of air, while the Peck family gathered around him, their faces growing longer and longer as they listened to his words.

9

In which a
Surprise or Two is
sprung and Thursday
gains his Spurs

It was Thursday who eventually found Harris. The first flakes of the winter's snow were already falling when he stumbled over him lying in a hollow beside a tree not far from Baron Munchen's estate. His limp body, one leg strangely doubled up beneath him, was still clutching part of the rocket.

'Must have dragged himself here after he hit the ground.' Mr Peck, brought hurrying to the spot by the deep baying sound of Grandpa Aristide's conch-shell, bent down and tenderly felt the form on the ground. 'He's still breathing – but only just. We'd better get him to the vet at once!'

'The *vet*!' A murmur ran round the other mice as they assembled in a circle round the scene of the disaster.

Mrs Peck clutched her husband's arm. 'Do you think ...' she began. 'A Grumbly ...'

'Must be some good in him if he looks after animals,' said Mr Peck briefly. 'Stands to reason, Ma. Besides, it's our only chance. Don't see as we can do anything ourselves.'

'Poor, dear Harris,' exclaimed Mrs Peck. 'That it should happen to him of all people.'

'That's what comes of trying to tamper with nature,' said Grandpa Aristide gruffly. 'If voles had been meant to fly they'd have been given wings.'

'Accidents are no respecters of persons,' grunted Uncle Ponty, as he helped lift Harris on to an improvised stretcher made up of twigs and dead heather. 'Thank goodness we found him before the snow became too thick.'

'Vets want money,' said Uncle Washington soberly. 'What are we going to do about *that*?'

'Perhaps he'll take payment in kind,' said Uncle Ponty hopefully. 'A piece of cheese or some cake...'

'We're not all like you, Ponty,' replied Uncle Washington. 'In any case, where are we going to get any cheese? The larder's just about bare as it is.'

'If we stand here arguing about it,' said Mr Peck impatiently, 'we'll never get him there. Let's worry about paying afterwards. He'll freeze to death if we don't hurry.'

'My pearl!' cried Thursday suddenly. 'I'll fetch my pearl. Harris always said it might come in useful one day.'

The others exchanged glances. 'Thursday,' began Mrs Peck, 'it isn't really...'

Mr Peck caught her eye. 'Let him go, Ma,' he said as Thursday ran off into the night. 'You never know –

it might even bring us luck. Goodness knows, we could do with some.'

And so, for the second time that night Thursday ran home, and from the organ loft he ran all the way back to the house in the village where the vet lived, arriving there just as the others were making Harris comfortable on the doorstep, covering him with leaves to keep out the cold.

'We can't do any more,' said Uncle Ponty. 'We shall just have to wait. Wait and hope.' He looked up at the sky and shivered. 'Though if you ask me things are going to get a lot worse before they get any better.'

Thursday placed his pearl alongside Harris's bed. 'May I wait with him?' he asked. 'I'd like to.'

Mr Peck looked toward his wife and then nodded. 'There's no sense in us all staying,' he said gruffly. 'But take care of yourself.'

'We'd better get Grandpa back home,' said Mrs Peck. 'We don't want to get his wheel-chair stuck in the snow.'

'I'll leave you me conch-shell,' said Grandpa Aristide unexpectedly. He gave a loud sniff as he helped himself to a liberal pinch of snuff. 'Don't know as I want to hear anything until you get back with news of Harris. Give it a couple of blasts if you're in trouble.'

'Thank you, Grandpa Aristide,' said Thursday gratefully, and then he too gave a shiver as a sudden scurry of wind whistled past his ears. 'I think perhaps I'll get inside it. It'll help keep out the cold.'

As the others crept away Thursday gathered the few remaining pieces of dry undergrowth from beneath a nearby bush and then climbed into Grandpa Aristide's shell.

Gradually everything became quiet again and as he settled down for his long wait Thursday peered out at a world which was becoming whiter with every passing minute. Not even the faintest mew of a passing cat or the merest flutter of a bird in its nest broke the stillness.

Overhead the branches of the trees began to bow under the weight of accumulated snow and even the church clock, as it struck the hours, had a different, slightly muffled sound, as if not wishing to disturb the silent figure on the doorstep.

Several times during the night he climbed out of the shell and fought his way across to the porch, but Harris remained as still and lifeless as ever. Thursday's heart grew heavier as he gazed down at his friend, until at long last even he dropped off into a fitful sleep out of sheer exhaustion.

When he awoke he found to his surprise that it was morning once again. The sun was shining and he sat up rubbing his eyes against the blinding light reflected off the snow as he peered across towards the porch.

For a moment Thursday stayed as if transfixed, hardly able to believe his senses, and then he made a wild dive over the side of the shell and into the snow, covering the distance to the porch in a series of leaps and bounds like someone possessed.

For Harris had gone. Disappeared. Harris, the stretcher, the pearl, even the leaves which had covered him had all vanished. Only a slight hollow in the snow showed where they had been. That and a series of other hollows on the steps where someone or something large had stood.

Thursday stood for a while, undecided what to do next, and then he turned and made his way slowly and sadly down the path towards the road.

It took him some while to reach home that morning and even then a party had to go out and rescue Grandpa Aristide's conch-shell. For overnight the whole countryside had changed, familiar landmarks had disappeared, and everything as far as the eye could see was covered in a thick blanket of snow.

'Never mind,' said Mr Peck, when Thursday told them his news. 'You did everything you could. Can't do more than that.'

'I don't even know if the vet took him in,' said Thursday miserably.

'Must have done,' said Uncle Ponty encouragingly. 'Stands to reason. I don't suppose there was anyone else about in this weather.'

'I tell you what,' said Uncle Washington. 'We'll pop down to his hut when it gets dark and fetch his fishin'-rods. We can keep them up here for safety. I expect he'll be glad of them when he gets back.'

'I wouldn't if I were you,' said Mr Peck, looking out of the window. ''Ave you seen the weather lately? It's got worse again. I reckon we're in for another dose. If you ask me we're going to be snowed up good and proper.'

'I don't know what we're going to do for food if we are,' said Mrs Peck. 'The larder's practically bare as it is. We've always been Sunday fed in this house, too. Every day of the week.'

'Reckon it'll be Monday leftovers from now on,' replied Mr Peck gloomily.

'Things often get worse before they get better, Dad,' said Mrs Peck optimistically. 'Perhaps when the snow melts our luck will change, too.'

'Change it may do, Ma,' said Mr Peck grimly. 'Trouble is it may even change for the worse!'

Mrs Peck gave a sigh. 'I don't think it *could* do that,' she replied. 'I don't think it could possibly get any worse.'

But as that day passed and then the next, with still no news of Harris or any sign of a change in the weather, Mrs Peck's optimism began to grow noticeably less, and spirits in the organ loft cupboard sank lower and lower until even Uncle Ponty and Uncle Washington found little left to argue about. In fact, for once in their lives, they were in almost complete agreement.

'Something *must* happen soon,' said Uncle Washington, as he stood at the window one morning and peered out at the countryside. 'Things can't go on like this.'

Uncle Ponty grunted and tightened his belt. 'They'd better hurry up, that's all I can say,' he exclaimed. 'Haven't got any more notches left. Me trousers'll be fallin' off soon.'

'I must admit I could do with a square meal myself,' agreed Uncle Washington.

'Don't care what shape it is,' said Uncle Ponty feelingly. 'Just so long as we get something. Dreamt last night I went for a swim in a sea of gravy. Tryin' to get to an island made of roast beef. Got me feet stuck in some Yorkshire puddin'.'

Uncle Washington nodded distantly. 'Saw a black cat this mornin',' he said. 'I read somewhere that's supposed to be lucky. Can't think why seein' any kind of cat, black or white, should be considered lucky, but that's what they say.'

'I saw it too,' replied Uncle Ponty morosely. 'Blessed thing went and walked right under a ladder, and that's supposed to be unlucky. Can't trust mogs. Never did like 'em.'

Uncle Washington screwed up his eyes against the light as he peered glumly out of the window. 'What's that brown thing standin' outside the church door?' he inquired. 'Been there all the mornin'.'

'Don't ask me,' said Uncle Ponty in a disinterested voice. 'How should I know?'

'Looks like some kind of basket,' continued Uncle

Washington. 'Big thing whatever it is. Got some sort of label on the outside. Thursday seems to be havin' a good look at it. Got someone else with him. Can't make out who it is. Looks familiar.'

Uncle Washington craned his neck out of the window with growing excitement. 'It looks like ... except it can't be, of course ... on the other hand ... perhaps it is ... I don't know, though ...'

'For goodness' sake!' exclaimed Uncle Ponty impatiently, as he joined the other on the window-ledge. 'Make up your mind, Washin'ton ...'

Uncle Ponty broke off suddenly as he too stared excitedly out of the window towards the ground far below. 'Sufferin' blowlamps!' he exclaimed. 'I do believe you're right. I really do believe you're right.'

'We shall soon see,' said Uncle Washington. 'They're comin' in.'

'What's going on?' asked Mr Peck, hurrying across the room to see what all the commotion was about.

'Ssh!' Uncle Washington jumped down off the window-ledge and put a paw to his lips as the sound of a pat, pat, pat, *thump*; pat, pat, pat, *thump*, began coming up the stairs, growing louder every second.

'Harris!' cried the Cupboardosities in a chorus as the thumping stopped and a familiar figure appeared at the entrance closely followed by an excited Thursday.

'Harris!' exclaimed Mrs Peck, rushing forward to

greet him. '*Thank goodness!* I was beginning to think we'd never see you again.'

'Harris!' cried Mr Peck. 'Good old Harris. Three cheers for Harris!'

Harris, looking unusually pink about the ears as the hurrahs rang round the room, climbed to his feet and lifted one leg for all to see.

'Good gracious!' exclaimed Mrs Peck. 'What *have* you got there?'

'Blow me!' said Uncle Ponty, as the cheers and laughter died away. 'It's a wooden leg!'

'Looks like best oak to me,' said Uncle Washington, examining it with interest. 'Can't beat oak,' he continued knowledgeably. 'Dip it in creosote when you get the chance and it'll last for years.'

'Haven't seen one of those since old Uncle Joshua lost his at sea.' Grandpa Aristide nearly fell out of his chair with excitement as he leant over the side in order to get a better view. 'It got swept overboard in a gale. Luckily he didn't have it on at the time.'

'The vet made it for me,' exclaimed Harris proudly, as everyone gathered round uttering cries of admiration. 'Baron Munchen's going to fix a reel on it for me later on. It'll make a jolly good fishing-rod. I shall never be without one now.'

'We shall be able to go fishing again next summer,' said Thursday. 'Every day if you like.'

'Oh, Harris,' began Mrs Peck, dabbing at her face with an apron. 'Everyone. I don't know what to say. I'm so glad.'

'Best news we've had for a long time,' agreed Mr Peck.

'You wait until you hear the rest,' said Harris. 'You haven't heard anything yet. Tell them, Thursday.'

'I've won a prize!' blurted out Thursday, hardly able to contain himself.

The others stared at him in amazement.

'A *prize*?' echoed Mr Peck. 'What sort of prize?'

'It's a hamper,' said Harris. 'It's outside. And it's got biscuits and cheese and jam and cakes and all kinds of other things inside. Full right up to the brim.'

'I won it because I travelled the farthest in the balloon race,' explained Thursday eagerly. 'I've never had a proper address before and when I knew I was going to stay here I sent the label back and . . . and . . .'

'He must have travelled the farthest,' said Harris, 'otherwise they wouldn't have sent him the prize.'

'I'd like you to have it,' said Thursday. 'Then you can open up the shop again.'

'Just like it used to be,' added Harris. 'Before it was altered. We all liked it that way.'

'With the counters to polish,' said Thursday, 'and sawdust on the floor.'

Mr and Mrs Peck exchanged glances. 'I told you things would change for the better,' said Mrs Peck.

Mr Peck nodded. 'You did that, Ma. Must say I didn't believe you at the time.' He turned to Thursday. 'I don't know what to say,' he began. 'It's not often I'm stuck for words, but I just don't know what to say.'

'How about a chorus of "For he's a jolly good feller"?' boomed Uncle Ponty.

'Half a mo',' called Mr Peck, holding up his paw as the floor began suddenly to vibrate. 'Listen.'

'Carols,' said Grandpa Aristide, putting an ear to his conch-shell. 'Good. I like carols.'

'Oh, dear,' said Mrs Peck, brought back to earth with a sudden bump. 'If they're going to play the organ I'd better get the china away.'

' 'Pon my soul,' said Uncle Ponty suddenly. 'Do you realize what the date is? It's the twenty-fourth of December. Christmas Eve!'

'Tomorrow must be Christmas Day,' said Uncle Washington excitedly.

'Of course it is,' said Uncle Ponty, glaring at the other. 'If today's Christmas Eve, tomorrow must be Christmas Day. Stands to reason. You'll be tellin' us next the day after that's Boxin' Day.'

Mr Peck coughed. Things were rapidly returning to normal. 'We're going to be busy,' he said, rubbing his paws in anticipation. 'If we're going to open up the shop and serve everyone in time.'

'You can stay and help with the cake if you like, Harris,' said Mrs Peck. 'You're not going home in all this snow are you?'

' 'Course he isn't, Ma,' said Mr Peck. 'We can't have you sitting all alone in that old tin hut of yours,' he added. 'Not over Christmas.'

Grandpa Aristide thumped the floor with his stick. 'Isn't anyone going to join in the carols?' he asked, glaring round the room. 'We only get 'em once a year. May as well make the most of it.'

Even as he spoke a full-blooded roar from the church below caused the organ loft cupboard to shake and tremble in every nook and cranny.

Uncle Washington rose to his feet. 'I like Christmas,' he said.

'So do I,' agreed Uncle Ponty, licking his lips. 'Mince pies.'

'Holly,' said Uncle Washington, glaring at the other.

'Turkey,' continued Uncle Ponty unabashed. 'With puddin' and cream to follow.'

Picking up his blackboard pointer Uncle Washington paused for a moment as if he intended digging it in Uncle Ponty's stomach and then, after a supreme effort, he held it high in the air.

A moment later, above the basses, above the tenors, above the sopranos in the church below, above even the blasts from Grandpa Aristide's conch-shell in the cupboard itself, there came the sound of many voices joined in song. And of those many voices two stood out quite clearly above the rest as they gave thanks for their good fortune.

'I very nearly didn't have a Christmas at all,' said Harris soberly, during a pause in the music. 'I'm jolly well looking forward to it.'

'So am I,' said Thursday happily. 'We didn't have much of a one in the Home for Waifs and Strays. They let us stay in bed for an extra half-hour but there weren't any presents. Besides, it's my first one as a Cupboardosity – even if I am only an HON. TEMP.'

'You're certainly not a "temp.",' exclaimed Mrs Peck, overhearing their conversation. 'Not after all that's happened.'

'Or an honorary,' agreed Mr Peck. 'Honourable, more like it.'

He reached behind the sideboard and withdrew a large bottle. 'Kept some of Grandpa's tonic just in case we had any celebrating to do,' he announced, as he began pouring it out. 'Began to think we were never going to need it.'

'Here's to the shop,' said Uncle Ponty, raising his glass.

'Long may it prosper,' echoed Uncle Washington.

'Here's to Harris,' said Mrs Peck, raising her glass as well.

'And a special toast to Thursday,' said Mr Peck amid general agreement. 'A first-class Cupboardosity if ever I saw one. Success, long life, a merry Christmas, and may all your adventures be happy ones!'